A Kill for the Poet

A Chaser on the Rocks
Book 2

Simon Maltman

TO Joan
hope you enjoy it!

A Kill for the Poet

Simon Maltman

For My Mother

Prologue

I woke up to the sound of static. It was from the television that protruded from the long, white metal arm at the side of my hospital bed. I rubbed at my eyes and readied myself to sit up. It was then I remembered my two broken legs and I thought better of it. I gingerly stretched out the rest of my body, under the crisp white sheets. The room was dark, but not black. There was always a stream of unwelcomed artificial light from the hall, but I decided it was probably night-time, just the same. I turned my head to the side and soon went over to sleep again.

"I'm sorry to wake you," a voice said abruptly.

"That's okay," I replied instinctively, blinking and gathering my senses. "What time is it?"

"It's six thirty," replied an attractive young nurse with olive skin, taking my pulse and holding her stop clock in her other hand. I looked up at her face, as I allowed consciousness to fully return. I felt the slumber drain swiftly out of me.

"That's fine," she said decisively and passed over a translucent cup with three small tablets inside it. "Take these up for me please," she said, leaning over towards me.

I reached over and threw them back, swallowing them down with a sip of water. I sure missed having a proper bloody drink.

"Get some more rest if you like, doctors' rounds will be about eleven today." She nodded at me and held me in a look.

"Thanks," I said, pressing the controls for my bed, raising my head up a little. "I think I'll watch some telly."

"Enjoy," she said lightly and gave me a brief smile. As the door swung behind her as she left, I could hear the sound of gentle chatter and metal wheels rolling across the waxed floors. I lifted out my fresh TV top-up card and keyed in the number to the unit. I put in my headphones, leaned back, and waited.

***

I'm sorry, I should really tell you something about myself. My name is Henry Flynn and I am a writer. You might have read some of my stuff. I'm from Belfast and I've written under my own name and also been involved in some ghost writing for, well, some C-list celebrities. I wrote some westerns a few years ago too under the name A.D. Lefevre. No? They were a bit shit, I'd admit. Anyway, I was just about to get started on a new project, when Bam! I had been up at the Giant's Causeway, carrying out some background research, and I took a bad fall or something and ended up breaking both my legs. Bloody typical! I've been bedridden for a few weeks now and it's starting to properly do my head in. What it has done though is give me plenty of time to write. I've been scribbling pages and pages, hour after hour. The problem is—it's all crap. I had been commissioned the job to finish off someone else's novel—write the ending and just do a good old tidy up generally. There was only really a first edit done by the guy it seems. The poor sod threw himself off the Causeway before finishing it. It's called *A Chaser on the Rocks*. That's why I was up visiting there. The publisher was keen for me to get started right away, but I wanted to get a feel for the project first. The trouble is—I haven't. This character of his, Billy Chapman, he's a 1940s PI, likes a drink, a good sort and all the rest, but I just can't seem to get a handle on him. I don't know what it is. I'll try yet again, after some toast and coffee, but a bit of BBC Breakfast News first.

***

It mustn't have taken long for me to drift back to sleep—maybe it was the pills they were giving me. I came to, just as some horrible bargain hunting programme was starting after the news. I must have dozed off for an hour or so, really must be those frigging pills they give me. There was a lukewarm cup of coffee, a carton of orange juice, and two slices of toast beside me. I wolfed it all down and felt better for it. I switched off the box, adjusted myself to a slightly higher position, and got out a new notebook. Right, time to start again, I decided.

Nothing.

I was determined not to write more shit. I had pages and pages of mediocre rubbish as it was. I looked up at the ceiling and watched as a daddy longlegs swung across it and onto the top of the windowsill. I looked up at the window. I couldn't see anything from my angle, apart from the occasional cloud passing by.

Then it struck me!

I don't know where the thought gestated from. I had been trying my hardest to find the voice of Billy Chapman, but I had barely evenly considered the voice of Brian Caskey, the dead writer. I'd never find the right pitch until I filtered through Brian first. Spurred on by this thought, I got out all of my notes on Caskey and re-read every one of them—slowly, one at a time. I gobbled up as much information as I could and tried to *feel* like him. I'm a ghost writer, so it might be cheesy, but I suppose I wanted to raise him from the grave. Then my pen burst into action and I wrote and wrote. Eleven thirty came and went and another nurse told me the doctor wouldn't be around now until the afternoon. That was fine, more time to write. My lunch was delivered, but I hardly looked up, my pen furiously finishing off another page of A5. On and on it went and it felt good. It was nearly four and I had been writing for most of the day when there was a light tap on the door. I neglected to react at first.

"Good afternoon, I hope I'm not interrupting you."

I looked up at my doctor, who had just entered the room, closing the door behind her.

"Oh sorry," I said, setting down my pen on my notepad. "I was a bit engrossed," I offered with an apologetic smile.

She walked unhurriedly towards my bed and sat down on the chair beside me. She was maybe in her late twenties, with long brown hair, tied up in a bun. She was pretty, with an easy disposition, dressed in white, with a stethoscope draped beneath her hair.

"I'm sorry I was so late getting to you," she said gently, crossing her legs and placing a black file across her thighs. Her black trousers pulled up slightly, revealing an ankle bracelet that distracted me for a moment.

"There was a multi-disciplinary meeting today, it took a little longer than expected and we talked for quite a while... about you actually."

"Oh," I said, repositioning myself against the hard white pillows that were propping me up on the bed, "I hope it's nothing bad."

"No, no, not at all," she said, gesturing lightly with one hand as if conducting the cello solo of a string quartet.

"There's nothing worse with my legs?" I pressed, feeling a prick of anxiety.

"No, there isn't. But, well," she paused, "we do need to speak about that too."

"Okay," I said evenly and clasped my hands upon one another.

"We've decided that it is the right time to talk things through with you now," she paused again, "Billy."

She looked up at me after the final two syllables.

I screwed my face up. "Billy?" I said smiling. "I think you mean Henry."

I was bewildered that after all these weeks she would get my name wrong.

"No, Billy," she said gentler still.

I stared at her, my mind blank, not knowing what to say. I actually felt bad for her and hoped she wouldn't be too embarrassed, she seemed quite muddled.

"Your name is Billy Chapman. You are in Knockbracken Hospital and have been here for several weeks now."

I smiled, still calm and almost amused. "No, I'm Henry and I'm in City Hospital because of my two busted legs."

"There's nothing wrong with your legs Billy," she said firmly.

I was starting to feel irritated, but still smiling through my teeth, I said, gesturing to my legs, "I have to disagree—there they are, both broken, I think that I would know that. And, please stop calling me Billy."

She gave me a sympathetic smile, but it grated on me. She rose and slowly pulled the starched sheets down from my legs. There they were, straight, clothed in blue pyjama bottoms and quite healthy looking. No bandages, no breaks. I stared at them, as if they had been transplanted from someone else.

"When were the casts taken off? Why do they look so... normal? I don't understand, the nurse must have taken off the casts when I was asleep. They must be doing better. You must remember who I am. Look, what's going on?" My voice was strained and began to crack.

A haze appeared just out of my peripheral vision and floated across my eyes.

"As I said," she continued tolerantly, "there has been nothing wrong with your legs and this is not a medical hospital Billy."

"Stop calling me Billy!" I blurted out hastily and then a memory pricked my brain. It was something unpleasant and unwanted—an obtrusive thought.

"I am afraid you came to us after having quite a major breakdown up at the Giant's Causeway. I'm sorry to say that you have been very confused. You passed out certainly, while you were there at the cliffs, but didn't suffer any injuries, well at least not physically."

She stopped and assessed my reaction. I didn't feel much at all, I've no idea how my own face must have looked, but her expression showed concern. She continued cautiously.

"It seems that you had created a persona, someone called Brian Caskey."

Caskey? I knew that name. Sure it was the author, but something else. I searched my memories with difficulty, my head hurt already; it was like trying to remember the registration number of an old car.

"Since you have been with us, you have developed another persona, this Henry Flynn," she added.

My head heaved finally into a migraine and my brain began to jolt about inside like a badly fitted car seat. I blinked a few times as spears of light penetrated my sight. I shut my eyes.

"You're wrong," I said quietly and squeezed them tighter still. I clenched my fingers into fists. I knew she was telling the truth.

"I'm sorry," I heard her say, before I lost consciousness.

Chapter One

Seven months later

"She cried and I held her and we felt close to each other. We smoked a few cigarettes and she walked me to the station. I didn't want to wait around and make things harder. The Causeway weather was more forgiving that day and it was a pleasant walk in even more pleasant company. She had thanked me earlier and I didn't care about that. What I cared about was that she was going to be okay. There wasn't much else for us to say to each other, but that was fine and it was comfortable. I felt a bit like Benandonner, ripping up the Causeway behind me.

"'See you in the funnies,' she said."

I paused for effect.

"That's the end of the reading, thank you."

***

I closed over the book and there was the sound of applause. A group of about sixty people were clapping politely in the Crescent Arts Centre, but it could have been about twenty thousand cheering at the Oval after I sank a winner against the Blues! I smiled widely. The clapping continued for maybe eight seconds and I leaned back from where I stood in front of the microphone stand, and looked out at the faces. My checked shirt felt sweaty at the armpits and my chest was a bit tight, but frig me I felt exhilarated. I was glad I had taken an extra pill at dinner time to keep me calm. Shit, better say thank you, I remembered.

"Thank you, thanks very much. I appreciate it," I said, leaning into the microphone.

The Arts Centre Director stepped onto the stage from the side, gave me a wink and took the mike out of its holder.

"On behalf of Crescent Arts, I'd like to thank Brian for being with us tonight and for the excerpt he just shared with us. *A Chaser on the Rocks* is out now and Brian will be signing copies afterwards. Thank you all for coming and I hope you have enjoyed the evening."

Therein followed another middleclass smattering of applause, but to me it was, "We're not Brazil, we're Northern Ireland," I'm David Healy scoring against England! I permitted myself another smile. I looked around the room again and saw many familiar faces. I didn't know them all and was pleased that some strangers had come along for my reading. It had been a rough year, fucking terrible at times, but I'd savour this. I definitely didn't recognise the solitary figure standing at the back of the room, to the right of the double doors. He caught my eye, as the applause eased to a trickle. He was average height, late thirties maybe, with a well cropped goatee beard. He was dressed in a smart jet-black suit, with an expressionless face staring back at me. He slowly turned on his heel and left through the back door.

Chapter Two

A punch in the guts is always a punch in the guts. It hurts. It stunned me for a moment and as I bent over double, my reflex was to spring back up again. I hit him hard on the nose with a right and a spurt of blood flew out and fell on to the polished hard floor. His head snapped back and he glared at me, his green eyes bulging.

"Don't you ever try that again," I said coolly, "You've no call to rough me up."

"You're a grubby little git and I don't want to see you within a mile of this station again, you hear?"

"I hear. I won't be solving any more of your cases again then I guess. So long Captain."

Chapter Three

As I was having a piss, I relaxed my body, no longer on display, and grinned inanely at the mirrors above the urinals. I was alone and let myself enjoy the satisfaction that the evening had gone well. I had been shitting myself for weeks and this was the first public event-type thing I had ever done. I zipped up and washed my hands at the sinks, as a sharp smell of bleach hit my nostrils. My mind flitted back to my recent stay back in Knockbracken Mental Health Centre and I only let the thought of it linger for a moment. It gave me a sickly shudder. There's something horribly unnatural in those places about the sterile smell of repeated cleaning and bleaching. I pushed it to the side, with my new-found confidence, and checked my cigs were in my jeans pocket. The door opened and a plump middle-aged man in a green and red striped polo shirt came in. He glanced at me on his way to the second cubicle. Sensible man I thought, I always opted for at least the second or third door—I've been in too many men's rooms over the years where I've washed my shoes in someone else's piss. He stopped and looked at me.

"I enjoyed that," he said warmly. "I'll have to get a copy."

"Thanks," I replied and when he closed the cubicle door, I beamed.

Chapter Four

The tobacco smoke floated over the glass and I took a cool sip of whiskey and rinsed it through my teeth. I eased back in my comfy chair, home and safe in my flat. I was still angry though. I didn't care that much at him losing his temper in the argument and whacking me. It was the principle. I had busted a gang of looters and all he could think about was that I had kept him in the dark a little. George McParland—a good enough police captain in South Belfast, but a terrible human being all in all. I suppose I had kept him in the dark a lot and I had made a bit of noise while I broke the case, but still. Short memories some people. It wasn't long ago I had brought in a Nazi spy for them and solved a murder at the same time. I took another drink. I let out a sigh and felt better. I put on a Leadbelly record and listened to his deep growl as he asked the ether, "Where did you sleep last night?" I took another slug of my drink. Fortunately, I'm not much of a dweller. I'd get my cheque for the private angle the next day—I was working for a local brewery. I had another few jobs in the works too. Things were okay, I supposed. Still, I wondered how Mary was keeping.

Chapter Five

I breathed in smoke hungrily. The first taste was foul, but the second hit the spot. I couldn't wait to get a drink soon too. There were a few others who had stepped out of the foyer and into the fenced off smoking area and there was a buzz about the place. 'Teenage Kicks' was being piped in from a speaker somewhere and I felt like tapping my foot. I obviously wasn't as emotional as DJ John Peel—he had famously said it was such perfect pop that it had made him cry. I continued smoking and my good form continued too, as I glanced about me. You have to pen in the tobacco lovers these days—keep them outside and away from the rest of the population. 'No smokers, No Irish.' If you hung that sign on bars round the world, most of them would have to shut. We're the great emigrant country, so they say. There's not many big cities round the world where you won't find a 'Murphy's Irish Pub' or an 'O'Shea's Irish Pub' or what have you. In saying that too, now nearly everyone in Northern Ireland has scrapped their UK passport and got an Irish one. It's easier getting around that way since leaving the EU. More people want to leave the country as well, now that the ugly simmering of racism and xenophobia has spilled to the surface. Well, I suppose here, it was never that far away.

Stubbing out my cig, I clocked the man in the suit, finishing off a thinly hand-rolled cigarette, standing towards the edge of the area. I think he saw me too. He pressed the butt down in an ashtray and headed straight out towards the steps and onto University Road.

"Well done Billy."

I turned towards the gentle arm that had been placed on my shoulder. It was Mary. I wanted to smile, but instead gave a half scowl.

"It's Brian now Mary, please."

I lit up another number.

"Okay, okay," she said warmly. "Old habits, sorry."

"Thanks though," I said, "for everything."

"Don't go all sentimental on me now," she replied and snatched my cigarette. She took a draw and handed me it back. "But I am proud of you. Bloody hell—I miss those."

I killed it and shrugged my shoulders.

"Now get back in there, mingle. Meet your fans!"

"Yeah, yeah," I said, moving towards the doors, secretly buzzing to be going back inside. "They say, 'Don't meet your heroes,' these guys are gonna be pissed off."

"In you go, National Treasure," she said playfully, giving me a shove.

Chapter Six

Belfast was a mess. It was 1949 and four years hadn't touched the sides on what needed to be done after the war. It was a long, hard, and slow rebuild—buildings and lives both. Every time I set off in the morning, it saddened me just how much there was to do. I had a few coffees after a fry at my local spoon on the Newtownards Road. I sat and thought about the previous couple of years. They weren't good years for anyone. Yes, the war was over and there was a period of collective elation, but then the hard, slow work and grind had to begin. PI work all but dried up for me for a time and I had to take work on the side where I could find it—bars, labouring. The last couple of years had picked up and I went back to getting enough cases to keep the man from the door.

Not much was going on in my personal life either. One hundred and sixty thousand American forces had been and gone during the war period, maybe that was why not a single local girl would look at me. Those guys had introduced chewing gum and swing music to the local fillies. I could only offer a cigarette and some blues. I had been two sheets to the wind for too long as well and I tried to give the drink a knock on the head. I did for a while, but how can you be a self-respecting PI without a dram and a smoke? Maybe it would always just be the solitary life for me.

Chapter Seven

"Could you make it out to Ian?"

"Of course," I said, "but who's he?"

The older gent in the tweed jacket looked confused. "Well it's me."

My attempt at chit chat banter at the signing had bombed.

"Ha ha, of course, thanks for coming," I said, cringing.

He moved on.

I died a little inside.

"I really enjoyed the reading. I've already started into the eBook, but you can't beat a real copy," said an attractive blonde lady, maybe in her late forties, setting down one of my novels in front of me to sign.

Shit, I thought, *this is about the best night I can remember. Maybe this writer thing could take off; maybe it'd even get me women.*

"Nice to meet you, thanks for coming," I said, trying to sound at ease with this whole thing.

"Please make it out to Helen," she said and I started to write.

"Where do you get your ideas from? I really like the forties setting," she said.

"Oh I don't know really, I'm just interested in local history and I suppose my background in the police helps."

"Oh, well good luck with it all," she said, looking suitably impressed.

"Thanks," I said.

I didn't tell her that writing it had pretty much kept me sane or at least brought me back from the brink of being a total space cadet. It had been about a year since the

Causeway thing and a lot had happened. I had been taken into the institution with pretty much the clothes on my back and my laptop full of about half the chapters of what would become my novel. I was in some state and though I didn't remember much of the early days, seemingly I was pretty much off my rocker. Some state—maybe more accurately, a catatonic state. Six months in there and I was declared sane again and I had a novel in the can. Well, it was a bit more complicated than that. Still, it's a funny old life.

Chapter Eight

*A*t *eight p.m., I arrived at the Great Eastern Bar near Sydenham. There was a fundraiser on for the rebuilding of the Glens' home ground, the Oval.*

"A pint of bitter, please Jim," I said to the lean bar man in his late forties.

"Coming up."

"Hi Terry... Gordon..." I nodded around to some familiar faces. The old place was packed out, all local men who had followed the club man and boy. The fundraisers had been going well and the ground was on track to be opened again before the end of the year. The stadium had been obliterated by the Blitz, including forging a large crater right in the middle of the pitch. I have a few shares in the club and at an early holder meeting, it was touch and go as to whether the club would survive at all. Sheer determination got the job done, and a desire for this club, that had been supported by the locals since 1882, to rise up from the ashes. This was the same story for many businesses and social ventures after the war. There was a knife's edge for all of them and many never made it. The Krauts may have surrendered years before, and eventually the Japs, but we were all still hurting from the aftershocks.

"Billy, good to see you."

"How are you John?" I replied, taking the outstretched hand.

John Neil was one of the trustees for the Glens. I had known him as an acquaintance for years, and a little better through the recent fundraising. He was perhaps fifty, tall, slim and with a thin brown moustache. His still auburn hair had started to recede at the back, but most could only see this if he stooped.

"I'm doing, well grand, grand. It shouldn't be too long until we are back in the east and back from Grosvenor."

"I know it will be a day to celebrate. Distillery has been very good to us, letting us share the pitch and lending us their kits, but it's time to come home."

"Sure Billy, you're right, you're right. Look," he said, glancing around him and setting an arm on my shoulder, "I was hoping I would bump into you. I have something that may interest you, a bit of work Billy."

"Thanks John, I'd be glad to hear about it, cheers."

"Good, good," he replied distracted. "I think the event is about ready to kick off now, will you see me at the end then, and I can explain?"

"Will do John."

Chapter Nine

I suppose I should elaborate on a few things. That night on the cliffs of the Causeway, everything had turned to grey and everything had become strange to me. If I had become a Christian, I'd probably say I was born again after it. Though, there's much more chance of me having another meltdown than ever becoming a God-botherer. I didn't know what was real anymore. Mary, my ex-wife, had confronted me and something in my head clicked and I knew I wasn't exactly who I thought I was. I stood there as the wind and rain beat me and I dropped to my knees and longed for death. I had been on a slow decline for a few months by then and in one instant, I could see it all for how it had been.

The next thing I knew was a crisp white sheet and whitewashed walls and the smell of disinfectant. The revelations from Mary had changed me forever, but they didn't change me back to who I had once been. I still don't know who the real Billy Chapman was and I don't feel him within me. I changed my name after I got out, to Brian Caskey, because for good or bad, that's who I am now. That's who I had thought I was for a time and it was as much as I had for an identity. My memory has scratches running through it and they're not in straight lines. What I do know is I mostly feel like him. That's as good as it's gonna get and I have a peace with it.

And then there's Sean. My son. Mary told me how we had lost him, years before, and how this had prompted much of my decline, but I still couldn't 'feel' him. I have mourned for him and I've felt a loss for him, but I don't remember him. I know the pain should be greater, but I suppose it's just caused me pain in different ways, seeping through like a slow burning acid.

When I was released, I got good support, I have to say. I had a good doctor, good community support, and this time I let myself invest in it. It helps when you have good people about, the last time those two balloons, Nicola and Amanda, just made things worse.

I didn't want to go back to those dark places and I still don't. That's why I have to keep writing. It's one of my priorities to cope with my condition. I have something called a coping WRAP, it's a way of coping with life I suppose. My diagnosis isn't that straightforward—I'm not bipolar, OCD, schitzo. I have a fairly unusual form of amnesia for a start, I've encountered one psychosis episode after another and I realise I've mental health issues for life. I accept that now. One thing I should avoid certainly are severe stress triggers. That's a fairly broad thing to do, and difficult too. I'm not a PI as such and never really was. I'm not registered. But, I did used to be a peeler and I have taken a few cases over the years. The thing is, I seem to keep getting involved in that kind of shit. And the real problem is, I quite like it. I just have to be careful.

***

The morning after the reading, I woke up fairly fresh. I had only sunk a couple of whiskeys after the event and was in bed for one in the morning. I live in the same flat and I'm glad to still have a roof over my head. I got a bit of help in sorting out some of my financial problems, like not losing my fucking mortgage. It's another stress removed.

While a fresh pot of coffee brewed, I followed my routine of reading my WRAP, taking my pills, and smoking a cigarette. I think the order and routine helps as much as anything. I was down to three main anti-psychotic meds each day and Lorazees for periods of stress.

The sun was beating into the kitchen and I opened the door and put out the cat's food. Yeah, I've even got a cat now too. He's called King Buzzo and he's quite the unfriendly bugger, but he's okay with me. He padded in and started to nibble.

I got myself a slice of toast and sat up on my kitchen stool, thinking. I had another signing arranged in Belfast Books for that afternoon and needed to get a few photos taken for my publisher too. I had a friend to pay a visit to before that. I wanted to try and squeeze in a few hours of work on my second novel too. It was going to be a busy day, but that was all right for the 'new me.'

I was in the early stages of trying to work out what Billy Chapman would get up to next. I wasn't going to be the next Steven King, but was happy to be making a few hundred quid every couple of weeks, mostly from electronic sales. I liked the new identity too—most people outside of mental health services didn't know anything about my troubles over the previous couple of years. Those who knew me as Billy mostly accepted that an ex RUC man with a few problems may well change their name. Those who I wasn't close to and thought anything else, well fuck them. I don't have the baggage of too many close friends anyhow.

I was happy to be forging a new path and felt some peace that I had come through the worst. I still struggled not knowing what all had been real and what was fantasy. I'd remember a particular conversation and would dwell on whether any of it actually happened. The kid with the wristband, for example, was real. I was on a case and had discovered a body. I had found him, but there was no conspiracy with the wristband and drugs and fake charities and all that shit. That had been part of my breakdown. I had to try and accept that too, that I'd have to let the will to definitively know what was real and what wasn't, go. I suppose all of us have to do that sometime.

Chapter Ten

The pub was all but empty. Myself and John Neil kept the bar open, seated in a snug at the back of the pub. The old wooden table was more scored than children's desks in the room of a hated teacher. It was slightly sodden by the end of the night too and peppered with ash spilled from cigarette ends and pipes. The green fabric of the booth's upholstery clung to me and I was warm from the drink, bodies, and craic.

"Another nip Billy?"

"Why not, it's early," I said with a wink and John lifted the bottle of Gordon's and poured us both some. I was usually a whiskey man when on shorts, but he was buying, so I would have to keep him company. He added a tiny splash of tonic each.

"Don't want to drown it," he said, his tobacco stained moustache breaking into a small grin. I hadn't seen him half cut before.

"So, what did you want to talk about?"

"Ahh," he said, lighting his pipe and pulling in small puffs to keep it going, "there is an acquaintance of mine who may be able to send a bit of work your way."

"I'm listening," I said, lifting my wallet and shaking it, feigning that it was empty.

"Good, good," he said and took a drink. "His name is Mervyn McBride. I don't think you know him?" he asked, raising an eyebrow.

"No, the name doesn't ring a bell."

"He approached me for some help and I thought of you. He is a 'Glen Man' himself and I first met him at a few social gatherings. He has a rather delicate matter involving

a theft of no small value. There are... complications and he does not feel the local police would be his best resource."

"I see, well I could certainly discuss it with him."

"Good, he hasn't told me more than that and he would indeed wish to meet with you. He also would want your discretion, which I know goes without saying."

He obviously thought he still needed to say it and it wouldn't be a problem.

"Of course. When would he like to meet?"

"Are you still using the office over on Belmont?"

"Yes, I'm still there, despite my enviable status. I'm really a philanthropist."

His eyes smiled as he let out a dark cobweb of smoke. "I'll arrange for him to call you tomorrow then."

Chapter Eleven

"Who have you come to visit today sir?"

"Tim Cairns."

The good-looking brunette, in perhaps her late twenties, brushed her fringe back from her eyes and opened a lever arch file. I looked up from the desk as men and woman healthcare workers in green uniforms pushed residents in and out of the lounge over to the right of me. Newly painted but white and bare walls stood throughout the care home. It was a joyless looking merry-go-round, that was only going to end in one outcome.

"Yes, please come with me."

She gave me an easy smile for free and led me down the white, sterile corridor. The smell of disinfectant was more overpowering than that of Knockbracken.

"I'll leave you two then," she said, after showing me into Tim's room.

"Thanks," I said, smiling at Tim as I turned, though taken aback by his appearance. The door shut and I needed another second to adjust to the change in him.

"Do I look that feckin' bad?" he asked in a coarse voice. He smirked. The coarseness had been due to his ill health, there was no bite in it.

"You've always looked fucking rough mate," I said and walked over to his bed.

I took a seat beside my friend who looked as if he'd aged at least a decade in the few weeks since I last visited.

"Here you go," I said and dropped a plastic shopping bag on his legs. He was seated, propped up in bed, the sheets half over him. He was wearing a Yardbirds T-shirt with navy tracksuit bottoms and his now grey hair still hung long, over his face.

"Oh, presents?" he croaked and heaved the bag up with a wheezy cough. He lifted out the contents, an issue of Classic Rock Magazine, a large packet of Tayto cheese and onion, and a bottle of Coke. The bottle's seal was broken and the contents were a golden brown.

"Cheers Brian," he said. "Oh," he added, registering the bottle, "thanks for the drink."

"No problem mate. So, how you been keeping? Pulled any hot nurses yet?"

"Any day I reckon. But here the doctor seems to think I'm doing pretty well, so maybe I'll have to bring one of them back to mine."

I winked at him and tried not to betray that I didn't really believe he would be getting out any time soon, if at all. I knew a bit how that was like. Shit, I've never been sick like Tim, but I knew something of what he must have felt.

"That's great news," I said. "We'd better keep you off that whacky baccy for a while still though."

"Aww," he said looking at the ceiling, "I'd love a wee smoke."

I grinned and stood up, taking a look out of the window. Cave Hill looked back, from a few miles away. The carpark outside was filled with mustard buses and a couple of ambulances. A few staff were huddled away from a thin spring shower, smoking against the back door.

"I'm sorry I missed your book thing the other night, how did it go?"

"Cheers Tim, yeah it was dead on. I think it went okay. Mary came."

"Oh, Mary went?" Tim said with a deliberately knowing smile.

"We're just friends," I responded with a shake of the head. "She's been good to me, helped me get over this last year."

"I know, I know, I'm just raking a bit," he said and then stopped for a series of persistent coughs. He gestured for his cup of water and I quickly passed it to him. He took a slow sip.

"That's better, so, what's next for you? Broadway? Hollywood?"

"I'm happy if I sell a few copies and most people don't reckon it's shite. It's good to get a few pound too. I'm hoping to maybe get a bit of work with the investigations alongside it."

"So you're just going to swagger around Belfast, like Clint Eastwood, big man in town?" he said winking and looked to be relaxing his painful body a little bit. He reached for the bottle of Coke, a sparkle in his eyes.

"Cheers," I said, nodding to him. "I'm aiming for Holywood, County Down. Man's gotta know his limitations."

***

As I drove out of the carpark, I noticed a black BMW idle past slowly on the other side. The man next to the driver made eye contact for only a split second, but I was sure it was the man again from my reading. We went on our ways in opposite directions and I shrugged it from my mind. "Have I taken all of my meds today?" I asked myself urgently. I had, it's nothing, just a coincidence, I told myself. The journey was only a short one. I sang along to 'Lazarus' off Bowie's final album, as I drove. Turning on to York Road, some apprehension set in. I practiced some of my breathing exercises and reminded myself that it was only a little signing, probably a couple of people at best. The main thing would be getting a few pics of my book in the window and that type of thing. I parked a quarter of a mile away, opposite the police station. It's probably about the safest place to park in North Belfast and even that wasn't a guarantee. I enjoyed the short walk, the rain gone and only sunshine left. I pulled out the e-cigarette I had been experimenting with recently and took out the oil. Bollox—I spilt some on my hands—the stuff was stinking. I had been trying to cut down on the smokes and it seemed like a good idea. Getting it sorted, eventually, I took a drag and made a face. I stuffed all the paraphernalia back in my jacket. I lit up a smoke instead and pretended I was Raymond Chandler, strolling around LA.

"Brian, good to see you."

I shook hands with the tall and burly store owner and we went out to the back of the shop for a coffee and a chat. A few of my books had been selling in his shop and he was certain that a couple of locals on the mailing list would make an appearance at some point. I spent the next hour at a desk with a pen and too many new copies of my novel. It wasn't an embarrassment and I should have been pleased. There were quite a few customers who showed an interest and three came down specifically. It still felt a bit like being the last hooker on display in Amsterdam's Red Light District.

***

At around three, I was at the desk and the shop was empty, with John the owner out the back. A man entered the store, briefly blocking the glare of the afternoon sun, only leaving an outline. When he stepped forwards and looked over towards me, I saw it was him again. He was in another smart tailored suit, this time dark navy. He swept the room with supple eyes. There was something about those eyes—they didn't dart, they were calm and thoughtful. This was a man in control. He sat down crisply on the chair in front of me and offered a thin smile. I smiled back uncertainly and gathered myself.

"Mr. Caskey, I am pleased to make your acquaintance."

I was taken further aback by a French sounding accent.

"Yeah, likewise. It's nice to meet my biggest fan," I said.

He feigned confusion, with a furrowing of his tight brow.

"Ahh, but of course, you saw me at your reading the other night? I am very sorry, it wasn't the right time for... for a little chat."

"You want to chat now?"

"Well," he said, wrapping his tongue tightly around the one syllable, "perhaps we could go somewhere for a cup of coffee afterwards, I am keen to discuss something with you."

I leaned back. Despite his charisma and persuasive manner, I felt confident enough and I admit my attention was well pricked.

"I'll need a little more than that Mr...?"

"Hertogen. Julien Hertogen."

"Well, Julien, my mum told me never to go anywhere with strangers. What's this all about? I'm guessing it's nothing to do with my literary prowess."

"That is correct," he said dryly. "It is some of your other skills that I am more interested in. I am aware of your abilities and your previous occupation. There is a task in which I think you would be well suited and I could provide you with a generous payment."

As I said, my curiosity was well pricked already.

I considered this and made a serious face.

"Have you ever had a pastie bap?" I asked.

Chapter Twelve

I awoke the next day with dog's breath and the stale smell of day old smoke in my bedroom. I had smoked a few cigarettes before bed. I had also permitted myself one nightcap. I hadn't needed them after consuming and inhaling enough at The Eastern. I probably should read a book before bed, but I didn't care to hear about handsome PIs with gorgeous blondes and exciting adventures. It was quite the effort to wrench myself from my sheets, but the morning light pouring through my curtains urged me to get up. You could spit through them, though I haven't tried yet. Two cups of coffee brought my senses around and there was some not-yet moulding bread to be toasted, that soaked up some of the liquid in my stomach. This new client sounded promising and I couldn't afford to miss him. I couldn't face the cycle to my office, and the walk through East Belfast was pleasant enough. I was happy to be getting to work again. I skipped my semi regular fry, figuring I'd save the money. Lean times meant some austerity measures. If things worked out, I'd have one the next day.

Chapter Thirteen

We sat at the back table in Galloper's Café, by the window. I hadn't been successful in convincing him into trying the local pastie bap cuisine and we both opted for a scone with jam and cream instead. He seemed to enjoy it okay, though I detected a slight grimace when he first sipped his black coffee. He was somewhat out of place in his suit and immaculate presentation, surrounded by older men reading the paper, and workers on their break in overalls and high-vis vests.

"So, you're not from around here," I affirmed lightly. "Whereabouts in France are you from?"

"I am in fact Belgian," he corrected, with no emotion. "I am from a small village, twenty miles south of Bruges."

"Oh, sorry, I'm sure you get that all the time, like Poirot."

"Excuse me?" he asked inquisitively.

"You know, people are always mistaking him, you know…"

His face was blank.

"Never mind. What is it you would like to talk about?"

He leaned forwards and took a brisk drink of coffee. He laid his hands in his lap.

"As I said earlier, I would like to pay for you to carry out a service. I want a man followed. I wish to know details of where he goes and who he meets. Is this a task you would be willing to perform? I do not want him monitored at a close distance or any approaches made."

"Yeah, it's something I do, but to have him tailed day and night, you need at least a team of three men for that."

"The matter is a private affair and I would not wish to involve others. I understand that there will not be full coverage possible. I am willing to pay £400 a day plus expenses. In exchange, I ask for daily updates and a full dossier on completion. For this price I also require discretion and a willingness on your part not to ask for any further details at this stage."

"I'll tail him for you. I'm happy to do about eight hours a day on it," I said evenly. "If things change and I don't like it, I'll walk away and just ask for what I'm owed up until then. There's no laws being broken by me if I just follow a guy for you," I said, tilting my head up, thinking. "If things change, I'd want more information from you."

"I think, Mr. Caskey, that we have a deal."

"Just one more thing," I added in my best Columbo. "Why are you asking me?"

He considered this and then straightened his coffee cup in its saucer.

"Let us just say that your reputation precedes you."

Chapter Fourteen

I swept my hand across the desk, pushing spilt tobacco, sweet wrappers, and crumbs into the almost full wicker bin. I hadn't been in for a few days and opened the only two windows to let out some of the mustiness. I looked out and stared across at the shipyard. The Nazi bombs had failed to take out the great old Harland and Wolff. I listened to sounds and shouts from the yard, brought across on the wind, a living part of East Belfast. It was funny to think that only a few months earlier, Princess Elizabeth and the Duke of Edinburgh were across there, visiting the harbour and smashing a bottle on the newest ship, The Aotearoa. I thought about that case in Antrim and the other that took me to Dublin and back. A lot had happened. Just like the war, it seemed a lifetime had passed since.

The first smoke of the day filled the void again. At five past eleven, I heard footsteps approaching the building. They shuffled on the front step and then the outside door creaked open. They moved up the old staircase, onwards to the small annex at the top. It's where a receptionist would sit if I had justification or money. I opened my office door.

Chapter Fifteen

That night I fell asleep, cigarette in hand, listening to 'The Winding Sheet' record by Mark Lanegan. The last track I remember hearing before dozing off, was the fantastically grimy cover of 'Where did you sleep last night.' Most people only know the later Nirvana Unplugged cover, but this version has Kurt and Krist on it two years before, a superior cut I think. I digress.

In the morning, I followed my routine, before a sour thought pricked me. What if I was confused again, imagining things? Even if I wasn't, should I be inviting this kind of stress in? No, I felt good, healthy. Well—reasonably, considering the drinking, smoking, and bad psychiatric history. It *was* real and I *was* in control. I wanted to see what it was all about and I wanted to know why I had been chosen in the first place. I could keep myself at a distance and it would be good for me to get back in the game a little bit.

The old Ford wheezed into action. Hertogen had gone on to describe who I would be following. His name was Davy Regan and he was forty-six years old. My Belgian patron had also given me a photograph—it was of a stocky, puffy faced man with receding black hair. I was informed that he lived in a flat along the Oldpark Road in North Belfast. I was outside in my car for half eight, smoking a cigarette and reading the Belfast Telegraph, subtly monitoring the front door as cool as Boggie himself. I had driven through a McDonalds on route and sorted myself out with a full McMuffin and a coffee. It 'aint no Ulster, but it did the trick all right. I felt good, poised. I took an extra pill, just in case.

It wasn't long after nine when Regan emerged. He was dressed in a green polo neck and black jeans, sporting an old Irish rugby cap. He appeared relaxed and beeped open a silver Audi and set off. I eased out into the traffic, after allowing two cars in first. The traffic grew heavy as we turned onto the Crumlin Road. We passed the gaol and crumbling old courthouse and I let another car pass in front. Three car lengths is fine when starting out on a tail, especially in slow moving traffic. He stopped off at a house on Squires Hill for about ten minutes and then came out again, still empty handed. I let a Beamer and an old Ka pass before continuing the slow pursuit. I had slipped back into my old work mode, the old knowledge still there, maybe a bit frayed, but okay considering all the shit of the last few years.

He pulled up again, this time at a new block of flats towards Mallusk. He went in for four or five minutes. Late morning, he pulled over at the KFC across from Yorkgate shops. I parked a few lanes away and after I saw him go up to the counter, I thought I should go in too. I also quite fancied some fried chicken and gravy. I was a few behind him in the queue and I made a mental note that he had ordered a Boneless Banquet. It's quite the meal for lunch and with the addition of no bones. Was he afraid of choking and an early death? Maybe just a greedy fucker. I sat near the door and watched him through the reflection in the window. He ate by himself; there was nothing to report, other than my dinner tasted pretty darn good. He was finished in five minutes and I waited until he was at his car before leaving myself, horsing down the last couple of fries.

He stopped twice more before crossing the Westlink and joining the carriageway towards Bangor. We both stayed in the left-hand lane, the midday traffic light. It only took half an hour to get to Bangor, both of us staying below sixty all the way. I even allowed myself a bit of music, tapping my wrist to The Posies for much of the way. When we approached the flyover, he kept straight onto the Belfast Road and took a right at the police station on Main Street. I was surprised to see him indicate left into the carpark by Castle Park.

That area is old Bangor. The Georgian mansion overlooks the town from the hill, a reminder of the lord and subject system that used to exist. It is now the town hall and base for the borough council. I remembered having to go on duty one night to help out the Bangor Police at the station round the corner. It was day after the first of two bombings inflicted on Bangor, by the IRA. Up until then, 'The Troubles' were twelve miles away in Belfast and beyond, though it had seemed like a hundred. After that, people knew that anywhere could be hit. I hadn't known the men I was on duty with that day, but I could tell they weren't themselves. There was tautness to their manner, a crack here and there, ready to break open completely. I was glad to get back to Belfast the day after. At least there, we all knew the score and had resigned ourselves to the daily unknown. I didn't understand how it was that I could remember things like this, but I couldn't remember a single day of my marriage or time with my family.

Regan turned past the town hall and went around the back, where he parked up. To the left, was Castle Park and the newly restored formal gardens, now open to the public. To the right, was North Down Museum, an annex of Bangor Castle. It is a small heritage centre with various exhibits and a nice café. I went there a couple of times when researching for what would be my first novel.

I parked a few rows away and waited. After a few minutes, Regan got out and went inside the museum. A shower came on and I watched as mothers rushed back from the park, wheeling prams, and children ran on beside them towards the shelter of their cars. A red squirrel darted across the grass in front of the town hall and scrambled up a tree. Usually it was only the grey ones you could spot. They're apparently the more aggressive and bully the red ones. No-one likes a Ginge apparently.

It was fifteen minutes before he came out again, got in his car, and headed back to Belfast. There were no more stops and he was home for the middle of the afternoon. I watched his flat for a few more hours and then went home. I called back past during the evening and stayed for half an hour. His car was there and there was nothing obvious to report. Hertogen rang me later and I shared with him what I had observed that day. He sounded pleased in an unimpressive sort of way and seemed to appreciate I had the detail of all the addresses etc. He was mostly interested in the stop off in Bangor, as was I.

That night I simply chilled in the house. I was still feeling good about things, positive, if you will. I say it because it is pretty noteworthy—it's not generally what people would accuse me of being. I skipped any drinking that night and had been trying to cut out having a few every day for a while. Lots of days there were far too many. I half watched some trash TV and did a spot of research for my new book.

I couldn't settle to getting a couple of chapters down, so I went up to my spare room and got the guitar out. It had been 'donkeys' since I had played it, but I was in the mood. I took up a coffee and Mint Aero and plugged in. A thick layer of dusk sat on top of it, along with everything else in the room. Not that there was much in the room—a badly cut old carpet, one chair, one amp, and a bookcase stuffed full of CDs, books, and DVDs. I've a few guitars knocking about the house, but the main one at the time was what I referred to as 'The Des.' It's a fake Les Paul, knocked off in China or Japan or somewhere. It cost me just sixty quid, but the thing is it actually plays really nice. Well maybe not necessarily the way I play it, or considering at any one time the most strings it ever has is five. One day I'd give it a clean and change all the strings. It'd be the same day I'd remember to check the oil and water in my Ford Fiesta before it overheated.

***

The next day was ground-hoggish. Some of the stops around Belfast were different, some were the same. The following day was similar again. What stood out was that each day he made a trip to North Down Museum. On the third day, as we pulled up at the museum, I had already made up my mind on the carriageway what I would do. Hertogen had said not to carry out any close observation, but I wanted to see where Regan went inside. I thought that it would at least help me start to formulate a few theories or give me something that I could use to get more information from Hertogen.

I waited two minutes and went and had a smoke outside the front door. There were only about a dozen vehicles out in the carpark, and looking through the old archway to the left, I could see most visitors were in the café beyond. I stubbed out my cig in the metal ash box on the wall and went on through the automatic doors, into the hall. The receptionist nodded a quiet hello and I repeated it back to her. There was no sign of Regan in the shop area. To the right was an exhibition about Saints Columbanus and Comgall and their missionary journeys from the Abbey in Bangor. I went through, stopping for a cursory look at each of the information boards.

I went into the adjoining room where it was decorated like a Viking tent. It was full of synthetic animal skins on the walls and ceiling, and there were cases with archaeological discoveries of swords and pottery. The five or so minutes I was there, I saw one older man reading some of the boards, and a caretaker passing through with a box of books and children's toys. That was it. When I was alone with the Vikings, I moved silently to the door and peered round the corner. I could see Regan in the next room, his back to me, standing beside an old piano. He went to turn and I crept back into the tent room, before he saw me. I pretended to read a display on the pillaging of Bangor Abbey and waited for a moment. I inched back to the door and could see Regan at the wall on the right now, stooping in front of a display of aristocratic looking folk with tennis rackets and ukuleles. He then walked to the far door and out to the small staircase, that led to the rest of the museum.

I entered the room and took in the signs entitled 'Percy French Exhibition' and 'The Percy French Society.' I stopped for a few seconds by the black Bechstein piano. Above it was a framed photograph of Percy and beside that his own watercolour of Bangor Town Hall. I casually went up the stairs and found the hallway empty. I went across to the main staircase and clocked Regan walking through the reception and out the door. He didn't look up. I carefully stepped across to the small arched window, overlooking the courtyard. I watched from the side as Regan got into his car and drove away.

I retraced my steps, back to beside the piano. There was nothing else in the room, apart from various displays and some paintings hung on the walls. I located the start of the exhibition and began to skim read. Percy French is one of those kind of olden day names you know if you're from Ireland, North or South. He isn't as well-known as a Yeats or a Lewis, but he is still pretty well loved. Just writing 'The Mountains of Mourne' alone gives him some recognition. I must admit I didn't know that much more about him, before going through the exhibition. He was an all-round entertainer, the display showed him in music halls, playing his ukulele, and in the deep country of rural 1900, with his easel and brushes. The Percy French Society seemed to have been responsible largely for preserving his legacy and it was all quite interesting. Music hall and trad aren't exactly my thing, but I could appreciate people remembering these artists that could easily fade into obscurity after a hundred years or so. There were photographs of posters for tours of Canada and the States too and a couple of handwritten notes.

What I couldn't understand was what some presumably criminal, middle aged guy from North Belfast was doing stopping off here day after day. I looked up at the ceiling and scanned across it. Walking to the door, I looked up over it and then climbed up the stairs. I spent ten minutes or so going around the quiet museum, examining where they had CCTV installed. From what I could tell, there were only five or six cameras, positioned above some of the doorways. It was an old system, the type that is still hooked up to video and records over itself every few days. It would be a good enough location to try and rob, but I couldn't see enough that would make the risk worthwhile. It could be somewhere for a discreet meeting I suppose, but though it was quiet, it wasn't very discreet. I also hadn't seen any sign of Regan meeting anybody.

I went down the stairs to the reception and leafed through a few books on Bangor's local history in the shop, giving my warmest open smile to the lady on the desk. She was a lady on the larger side, with blonde hair, maybe around forty. She looked like a bubbly kind of person, friendly—you can just tell.

"Can I help you with anything?" she asked with a warm, country accent.

"I'm just browsing, thanks. I haven't been here for a while and I'm enjoying the displays."

"That's good to hear, we've got a good little museum in Bangor."

"It is, I hadn't seen the Percy French display before, it's interesting."

"Yes, we keep all of the memorabilia here. The rest of the materials are available to the public on request.

Actually, there's a guy researching for a book at the moment, comes here a lot of days, you just missed him."

"Is there?" I said.

I told her I was going for another look around and I headed the long way around, back to the exhibition.

"Right, Caskey ya goat ye," I said to myself, "Think!"

I surveyed the room again. I didn't buy that Regan was working on a book, unless it was a local memoir on his life of crime. I turned on my heel and looked closely at the piano. 'Do not touch' was written clearly on a plaque resting on the keys cover. The other sign above it stated that the piano had been a gift from Percy to his eldest daughter, Mollie, for her 21st birthday. What was Regan doing here?

I was busting for a smoke, but I decided to stay a few more minutes and maybe I'd look in on his house again for an hour or two in the evening. I walked around the room a couple more times, generally just glancing at the displays again, thinking. I stopped once more by the piano. I checked through both doors quickly that nobody was about and then lifted up the cover of the keys. It looked in good condition, nice old ebony and ivory, that McCartney and Stevie would be proud of. I'm not much of a pianist and didn't press my luck by having a tinkle. I closed it gently shut again and stepped around to the back. I lifted up the hinge on the back cover above the strings. I looked inside. It was hard to see and I couldn't make out much. I reached down in and felt carefully about from left to right. My fingers touched paper. I grabbed it and pulled it out. I looked down at my hand with surprise at a twice folded over piece of lined A5 paper. I closed the cover back down shut. I looked up and listened like a meercat on patrol. All was quiet. I started to open it.

"The café has a cream tea offer on at the moment if you're looking for a caffeine fix."

"What?" I said, not managing to hide the start she gave me. I hadn't heard the receptionist come in, and she looked at me with concern.

"Oh, I'm sorry to give you a jump, whoops," she said, with a friendly chuckle.

"No, you're fine, sorry, I was engrossed. A cuppa would be great. I'll probably head round in a minute."

"Take your time, it's open till half four," she said and left.

I listened to her footsteps disappear down the smaller staircase. I let my heart have a second to recover. I opened the rest of the paper that I had been absently gripping like a teething baby on a soother. On it in blue biro was written:

91-hu677-s6-tyuh6-o5-67rrqw-006g-op-oop987-00

Chapter Sixteen

"Mr. Chapman I presume, pleased to meet you."

"Dr. Livingstone actually," I said, with a firm handshake and open smile.

"Aha, yes, pleased to meet you. Mervyn McBride," he responded awkwardly.

"Good to know you," I said, leading him inside. He was an overweight man in middle age, ruddy faced, with thinning grey hair.

"Please take a seat."

"Thank you," he said and seemed relieved to sit, panting lightly from the stairs.

"Can I offer you a drink of something, or coffee?"

"No, no, thank you," he said, in his all but RP voice, with just a texture of Belfast crackle.

After a bout of small talk, we got down to business.

"Mr. Chapman, you come recommended and I would like to involve your services in a delicate matter. I own several art galleries. My primary concern is based out of Newcastle—'Valley Collections.' I was exhibiting a collection at the Slieve Donard last week." He paused. "Sadly several works were stolen and have not been as yet recovered."

"What do the police have to say?"

He creased his brow and moistened his lips. "Unfortunately there are a number of factors requiring my wanting to handle this privately."

"You haven't reported it?"

"No, I have not," he said, catching my eye. "I wish to enlist you in investigating the matter, with discretion. If you agree to this case, I will provide you further

information and pay for your stay at the Slieve Donard in addition to your usual rates and expenses."

"That sounds fair," I said and began to light a celebratory cigarette.

"Good, good," he added and nodded with a thin smile.

"When would you like me to start?" I said, inhaling.

"As soon as possible."

"I can start today," I said.

Chapter Seventeen

Hertogen had agreed to meet me to discuss the day's surveillance in person in a new wine bar, off the Lisburn Road. He had wanted an update over the phone, but I needed to see his eyes.

"Good evening, Mr. Caskey."

"Brian," I said, sitting down in the wooden booth, where Hertogen already was halfway through a bottle of red.

"Please," he said, gesturing to the second glass.

"Thank you," I said and he filled my glass, as he held it up. Red wine always seems to give me great, big, bloody hangovers. Well, it wasn't an exact science, most times I drink, I have hangovers. But still.

"What is it you would like to say to me exactly?" he asked, raising the rim of his glass delicately against his lips.

"I found this," I said and pushed the message across the table to him. "It's a copy, I put the original back where I found it."

He surveyed the object, pursed his lips and looked up at me again. He fixed me with a stare, as he unfolded the paper.

"We had agreed on no close supervision," he said firmly, the first trace of emotion in his voice.

"Yes, but sometimes you have to play a hunch," I said simply.

He looked down at the paper, his eyes hooding as he absorbed the information.

"It's obviously a code," I said.

He didn't speak but fixed me another hard look. He shrugged and took a long sip on his wine.

"Can you read what it means?" I asked, Hertogen still silent.

He paused and looked down at the table as if he was examining the type of wood.

"No, but I could have it transcribed," he said.

"Good, now we're getting somewhere, you've got to meet me halfway here." I stopped and took a quick gulp. "What is it all about?"

"Mr. Caskey." He sighed. "Brian, I wish for our arrangement to continue and I would prefer the terms we agreed on. However, I am willing to share with you two things."

I gave my hardest stare back. I knew I had two pair, but he could be hiding big slick. He'd hit me on the river.

"Go on, I'm listening," I said, taking out my small silver lighter and fidgeting with it under the table.

"Very well. Firstly, I can tell you that I work in a diplomatic role for the Belgian Embassy."

"Okay," I said, but wanted to say, "no shit."

"It, how would you say, would be beyond my job role, this particular investigation. This is not... official, you might say."

"Oh, right, okay. But we're not breaking any international laws or anything?" I asked, mostly just to try for a reaction.

He feigned disappointment in me with wide, Orson Welles eyes. "No, no, of course not. It is, how do you say, only 'playing a hunch?' I am simply looking into some enquiries."

"Fine, what's the second thing?"

He leaned forward conspiratorially.

"It was no small matter that I chose to involve you in my little 'investigation.' You have been involved in a small way with a large puzzle that I am trying to assemble. Three degrees of separation. You discovered the body of a teenage criminal. He was wearing a white wristband."

My mind faltered and I almost gagged. I instinctively pressed my hand to my pocket to check I had brought my medication.

"This young man was involved with other criminals, one of whom you have been following for me. You were right in thinking there was more to his murder at the time. I understand that it was a troubling period for you," he said, pausing and briefly holding my gaze. "You may take comfort that there was indeed a bigger picture, though not the one you constructed. I cannot tell you anything further at this juncture."

I wasn't expecting any of that.

Chapter Eighteen

I left a sign on the door and a message with the grocers at the corner. It wasn't unusual for someone to ask Jack the owner about reaching me, when I was out and about so much. It sure didn't take up too much of his time either. I didn't anticipate any sudden crime spree or lost puppy epidemic, so if I was away for a week or so, Belfast should be fine and dandy. If McBride was happy to pay my board in a swish hotel, more power to him. I put off packing my bag by drinking in the afternoon. I smoked a packet too. It all felt good. It was kind of happy drinking. It made a change from the 'I've got no money and I'm lonely' drinking.

Chapter Nineteen

Hertogen had offered me some time to think things through. He said that he realised it mightn't be the kind of thing I was looking to do, but he also very much hoped that I would continue. It was only after nine when I got home and I took a few shorts to steady my nerves. Secret coded messages? Working for foreign diplomats. I had agreed to take the time and maybe pretended to myself that I would have to think about it. Hertogen said he could make arrangements for someone else to cover surveillance for a couple of days—of course he didn't elaborate any further. Of course I would stick with it too, but a few days' break to think things through I knew would help me keep myself together. I couldn't afford to get carried away or let my mind fuck about like last time.

I read through my WRAP and settled myself that I would spend a few days writing and chilling out. It always settled me and I was already in the throws of a story gestating and wanted to see where it would lead. I lit a smoke up and settled in front of Google with a cup of coffee. Within an hour, I had booked a decent one night deal for the following day at the Slieve Donard Hotel in Newcastle. I might as well write from memory. I had no real ties, the drive would do me good. I could throw myself into some research and maybe get some perspective on the Hertogen thing.

I was in bed by eleven and fell straight into a dreamless sleep. I woke at seven, followed my routine, threw a few things in a bag. I left three bowls of food and two of water out for Buzzo. I called past the shops to get a few things I needed, smokes in the shop, a few nibbles for the car too. I called into the wee pharmacy for my meds last, I didn't want to run out of those.

"What about ye Mark?" I said, squeezing past stands of shower gel and bottles of bleach. It seemed that chemists didn't make enough off just medication these days.

"Hiya Brian, there's our local celebrity," he said genially.

Mark was an affable guy, probably early thirties, thin.

"That's me," I said with a wink. "I'm breaking so many hearts you'll run out of anti-depressants," I added.

He laughed. "I must get round to reading that book of yours. What can I do you for?"

"Just my new script please," I said, looking over to the shelves behind him.

"Oh yes, no problem," he said and disappeared into the room behind the small desk.

"Here you are," he said, returning after a minute or two. "You'll need to get a new script from the doctor before the next lot, okay?"

"Ah right," I said. "I'll make an appointment, cheers."

I signed for them and headed back out into the cool sunshine. I made a mental note—I really should make a new appointment.

Chapter Twenty

I took the tram over to the city centre the next morning. I walked across to Great Victoria Street, carrying my small suitcase, a light drizzle wetting my hat. The train to Newcastle would be another fifty minutes, so I ingested both a coffee and a copy of The Tele in the café. The coffee was bitter and so was reading again about the slow progress of regeneration in the city. Rationing would continue, the pound would remain weak for a longer period than suspected, and the Glens had been beaten 2-1 by Belfast Celtic. That all, at the very least, gave my good mood a wobble. As I boarded the train though, I couldn't feel anything but optimism. It was enough, just to escape Belfast for a few days. I hadn't actually been outside its boundaries since the case up at the Causeway.

The bell sounded right on time, and the engines wheezed like blowing out the first cigarette smoke of the day. I don't think I had ever travelled in first class before, let alone had a carriage to myself. I was enjoying the view of leaving the Albert Clock and the Lagan behind, when the drinks trolley came around. I gladly received a glass of white and a copy of The Times. I mulled over both as far as the crossing from Antrim to Down, and my escape to the country. The drizzle had become a heavy shower and then the clouds parted and the sun streamed in through the small sash window, allowing a clear view of the rolling fields and occasional barn. As we approached Newcastle, the mountains appeared from out of nowhere. They drape above the town, like a fly holding an umbrella. It's quite the sight. Outside of the cities, that's where the poets and artists find their love for this island of Ireland.

Chapter Twenty-One

The long route to Newcastle, through County Down, is a much nicer drive than the mundane trip up the motorway. Down has history, it seeps through every ruin and forest. And there are plenty of both. The peninsula to the right of Strangford has a topography and an indescribable quality, that has barely altered for a few thousand years. Here you can still see and touch real history linked to druids, Saint Patrick, Vikings, earls and kings. Get me! I should really get a job with the fucking tourist board. I rumbled along in the rusty Ford, life feeling on the up. The sun was out and I needed my shades. With the window down, I smoked a few cigs and listened to Prince, 'The Rainbow Children.' It's an awesome album, very underrated—good funk on a drive can't be beaten with a big stick. I stopped in Downpatrick for a coffee at the St Patrick Centre. The café is on the roof terrace, with the cathedral in the distance and Paddy's own Saul Church one mile away. It was enough caffeine to take me the other miles to Newcastle. I went straight across at the crossroads via Castlewellan and on through Dundrum.

When I haven't seen the Mournes for a couple of years, they never fail to stagger me. There is something incongruous about such a huge mountain range towering over the top of a small village, in little Northern Ireland. It's no wonder that they have inspired so many songs and poems. 'Black Rose' popped into my head, Thin Lizzy's homage to Ireland's cultural history. It quotes Percy French and how 'The Mountains of Mourne wash down to the sea.' Everyone gets a mention and many classic Irish ballads lend a refrain or two. They're all there—Yeats, French, Wilde—even Van the Man and Geordie Best!

I adjusted my eyes to the road again and missed the turn off for the hotel on the way into the one-way system. "Shite," I said under my breath, stuck going the wrong way. I was in no great hurry and idled on through the town. Newcastle never changes much, and always looks better on a sunny day. It's filled with cafés, bucket and spade shops, pubs and arcades. It's not quite Blackpool and all the better for it. They've done a nice job of developing the promenade and they've kept much of the old Victorian, sea-side charm. As I was pulled around the one-way system, with the other cars, like metal shavings by a magnet, my mind flitted to the case. "Remember your WRAP," I repeated to myself a few times. I needed to keep my head in all of this and not let myself get too stressed. "Just go easy Brian." I headed back to the roundabout and out to the turnoff for the Slieve Donard Hotel. I caught it this time.

Chapter Twenty-Two

The station at Newcastle is a grand red brick affair. There's an impressive clock tower, that was added in the early part of the century, offering Greenwich to the many commuters passing through. It was bustling when I arrived, businessmen and assorted travellers making their way in and out. I felt suddenly wide awake after the sleepy train ride. A train journey lets you have a little bit of precious time to gather your thoughts sometimes and to prepare for whatever purpose your journey served. It's a nice way to travel. It's a shame that within ten years, this station would be closed, along with much of the once great Irish Rail Network.

I walked on through the upper part of the town, smoking, I hadn't been in South Down since I was a child. I found myself in a lively town centre, full of busy shops, coal sellers, postmen, women with prams, dogs. There was also the familiar seaside waft of dulse and other seaweed, coming in from the sea. Some people don't like it, but it's the smell of holidays to me. There would be many buckets and spades working over that beach before the season was done, and many an ambler across the mountains too. I had never set foot in the Slieve Donard Hotel, but was awestruck as a child, when I passed outside it once. I felt something akin to that again, as I stepped up to the bold black gates surrounding the huge building.

Chapter Twenty-Three

The hotel façade is almost as impressive as the approach to The Mournes. It's probably just shy of ostentatious on the outside and guilty of it in places within. Built by the railway men in 1898, it was and is a luxurious tourist location. The one hundred and twenty guest rooms are still there, but the smoking rooms and billiard rooms are long gone. It wasn't the billiards I'd miss.

I entered through the large revolving doors, first stubbing a smoke out in a hefty metal ashtray resting on a wooden bench. The reception was tranquil, everyone seeming to know where they should be and what they should be doing. The décor was all from a gentle pallet, very plush—though shit, what do I know? A pretty brunette, with her hair tied back, checked me in and sent me on with a porter to my suite. I hadn't detected any stuffiness that my stay had been a cheaper last minute deal. I admit I never feel really comfortable in those places. I gave the porter a quid and got myself settled in.

The room was immaculate and spacious. There was a shower, bath, and bidet in the tasteful en suite. I'd probably use both the bath and shower, but I had no interest in jetting a fountain of water up my hole. Crucially, there was a balcony off the bedroom, where I could smoke. All was well in the world. I checked the teas-maid, plenty of coffee and milk sachets. It's top of the list when us Brits are rating somewhere. Maybe that's the reason we left the EU. The other Europeans don't go in for the traditional British teas-maid so much. I could never think of any better reasons why people wanted Brexit.

Chapter Twenty-Four

The brickwork looked as if it had been pressed against the drying cement only days before, it was in such good shape. The overall impression was that of an old elegance. The inside was the same, modern sophistication with timeless class. I made my way to the large reception area and, after checking in, went up to my room. As soon as I entered, I felt like a different man. Getting away from Belfast again was just what I had needed. The war had changed me and leaving the war had changed me again. Now it was time for something else.

Chapter Twenty-Five

I set my laptop down at the writing desk. There was headed paper and compliments slips sitting on it. I'd have to write myself some notes, feel like Hemmingway in his hotel on the Seine. I worked through the afternoon, and got almost two thousand words down. They weren't all that pretty, but sometimes getting the proverbial words on the proverbial paper is a start. I raided the teas-maid and had a couple of smokes on the balcony, and was feeling good.

It was maybe five-ish when things changed, and a sparkle of light danced off the screen and onto my eyes. I tried to blink it away, vainly. I knew the all too familiar first seconds of a migraine and laid my hands out in front of me. Sure enough, half of my fingers had dropped away. Fuck! I hadn't had a bad migraine for maybe two months.

I closed the screen and went in search of my paracetamol, before it came on fully. Crossing the room, I closed the blinds, my vision starting to cloud over further. I took two tablets and strained to pour a glass of water. I pulled myself up onto the bed and shut my eyes. Light danced over my eyelids, trying to get in, and a thumping pain pulsed at the back of my head. I opened my eyes for a second and all of my sight had gone. Shit. It was a wash of colours and refracted light. I buried my head into the pillow and hitched up my knees. I attempted to calm myself, but I hadn't been feeling any great stress. I suppose the case was playing on my mind some, maybe it was a mistake to get involved. Nothing could be done but wait it out, maybe sleep it off. The heavy thud carried on inside my brain and I could sense a light show going in full flow, outside my eyelids. Maybe it was just my body wanting to know what I had decided to do. 'Stop procrastinating,' it was saying, tell us what you're going to do. Of course I was going to follow the case through, I'd just take it easy. I would ring Hertogen the next day, once I was back in Belfast. But I wanted the chance to make the most of the stay. I needed to shift the stupid headache. I forced my eyes closed even tighter and tried to sleep.

***

Eventually sleep had come. A cold, unsettled sleep. When I awoke, the room was dark, but there was light beyond the blinds still. I hesitantly opened my eyes. Things were still blurry, but the migraine had passed. My head still throbbed. It felt like Barry McGuigan had been practicing on it. I checked the time on my phone—8.46 p.m. Bollox, the trip hadn't gone the way I had wanted. I had envisioned an early evening walk and then a meal in some restaurant or another that I would happen on along the promenade. All very civilised. Fucksake. I got up slowly and felt a small head rush. My stomach pulsed, I was hungry too. Ravenous actually. I always felt half bloody starved after a migraine.

By nine thirty, I had showered, drank a cup of coffee with two more paracetamol, smoked, and hit the stairs. The bar was quiet. It was a cosy, yet fairly opulent set up with booths on two sides, all with sea views.

"Bushmills on the rocks please," I asked of the innocuous barman.

I eased into a booth with my drink and a menu. The kitchen had stopped serving meals for the night, but they could do me up a plate of sandwiches, he had told me. I got some egg and onion. They came after twenty minutes and were friggen lovely. I don't know what they had done with this pretty regular pairing, but it was bloody great. Maybe it was the fact I was so hungry and the food eased my headache some. After a packet of bacon fries and a pint of Guinness for desert, I felt almost normal. Well, maybe the kind of normal like when at a party at three or four in the morning, you get a second buzz on, but your hangover starts as well.

Chapter Twenty-Six

I was laid out on the bed, smoking, when the knock came. I stood up and pressed on my shoes. I answered the door to a prim, young houseboy.

"Mr. Chapman, I am very sorry to disturb you. There is a Mr. Fotheringay arrived to see you in the drawing room. He said to pass on that he is an associate of Mr. McBride."

"Thank you," I said opening the door a little wider. "If you could tell him I will be down presently."

"Yes sir, good evening."

"Good evening," I replied and shut the door. I glanced around my finely decorated room. I had never stayed somewhere like that before. With some sadness in leaving it alone and that comfy bed, I grabbed my smokes, hat, and room key, and made my way down the grand staircase.

Entering the grand panelled drawing room, I met the gaze of a lean figure, resting lightly against the main bar. He was tall, middle aged, and dapper. He had a pencil moustache and busy eyes.

"Mr. Chapman, allow me to buy you a drink," he said and patted me sharply once on the back.

"Mr. Fotheringay?" I asked, instigating a handshake.

"Yes, I manage Mr. McBride's local gallery," he replied in a priggish London accent, clasping my hand.

We sidled over to a table with a fine sea view and a young waitress took our drinks order. We both had a brandy and chased it down with a sweet sherry. I took his lead. It was kind of fun. This fella was used to gentlemen's clubs and gentlemen's drinking. Once we had moved onto shorts, he began to fill me in about the case.

"It was a sad thing to happen Chapman," he said soberly, while puffing on a thick Henri Winterman. "Not nice this type of thing and I'm afraid there were... complications."

"What was stolen exactly?" I asked.

"There were five paintings taken in all. One was by far the most valuable, a work entitled 'The Hound of Ulster.' It is a watercolour of a standing stone in Conlig, County Down. It is a very valuable piece, surely the main objective of the theft. The scene involves one of the tales about Curchulion. Do you know it?"

"I don't think so," I said, lighting up another number.

"Legend tells us that the young warrior, the 'Hound of Ulster,' left that great stone there, following a battle with Benandonner. Seemingly, Benandonner had come back for another fight, Finn McCool mustn't have given him enough of a scare," he snorted, taking a drink of his scotch and water.

"No, I'd never heard of that. So, was this a special collection of paintings that night, were they all by the same artist?"

"Oh, I'm sorry," he said blinking and sipping his drink, "I thought you were aware that the thefts were all from the French collection."

"French? Percy French?" I asked keenly.

"Yes, that's correct."

The name wouldn't resonate particularly with most people, but it had significance for me. Everyone knows Percy French as a performer and songwriter, but lesser so as an artist. I had followed his rise as an artist, sadly only really doing so decades after his death. That wasn't what made it resonate with me though. I had met him once. In 1920, I was only a teenager and I had a summer job as a *bus boy in the Grand Central. It was the grand old dame of Belfast, attracting all sorts of famous guests through the years like even King Leopold of Belgium. I never met him though, or saw any pictures by him, if he drew any. Anyway, Percy French had stayed for a few days and I had been attached to him—pressing his suits, bringing his drinks—that type of thing. He was kind to me, asked me about myself, took an interest in a working class dogsbody kid from East Belfast.*

On the last day of his stay, he had been booked to perform in the main ballroom. It was a sixteenth birthday celebration for the Lord Mayor's eldest daughter. I watched the show from the wings and he was terrific. He had the audience in his palm, a gentle confidence keeping them entertained and engaged through both story and song. At the end of the performance, following an encore of 'The Mountains of Mourne,' I had a clean shirt and a brandy waiting for him, before his reception with the main guests. He offered me his hand and thanked me for looking after him so well during his stay. He said he would be leaving early the next morning and apologised that he did not have his wallet as he had wanted to give me a parting tip. He snatched up an off-white linen napkin and began to mark it with his pen. After a few seconds, he flipped it over, displaying a rough sketch of a face. It was mine. We both smiled. He turned it back and wrote on it again for a few seconds. He handed it to me and said goodbye. I opened it out and read what he had written underneath the doodle.

'I have just finished a children's party, I am one of the few survivors.

Thank you, Billy.
Yours,
Percy French.'

I still have that napkin, in my old pine box with other keepsakes, love letters, and memories. It's a pretty shallow box.

Chapter Twenty-Seven

The breakfast was good, really good actually. As we say in Belfast, I beat it into me. I had to check out by eleven and was packed up in good speed, leaving time for a second pot of coffee. I enjoyed milling around the hotel reception and lounge area, and by a quarter to, I had settled up and was back in my trusty old Fiesta and heading through the town and out towards Silent Valley. I parked beside the visitor café and, in two minds, settled on stopping for another caffeine fix. Afterwards, I walked over to the grassy banks and down to the long, winding road up to the dam. It's a beautiful spot—the sky was a clear, light blue and there was only a mild breeze over the motionless lake of water. I took out my e-cigarette and thought I'd give it another blast. Bloody stuff went all over my hands again. I got it going soon enough but it tasted rancid. Well, I had tried. I took all the paraphernalia out and shoved it in a bin. That was that.

It took me almost an hour to walk and smoke up to the dam itself. It's bloody huge, like some unworldly structure out of Lord of the Rings. Seemingly, everything around Newcastle was on a massive scale, well maybe not the night life. I felt peaceful. I was ready to be challenged; I'd cope with whatever life would throw. Well, maybe. I turned on my heel and headed back towards the car park.

***

I had bought tickets months previous, for a concert that night in Belfast. It was to see The Blind Boys of Alabama. I had time for a shower and shave at home before heading out to Belfast's Waterfront Hall. On the way, I stopped around the corner at Giant FM.

"Yeah, I've got ten minutes, I'll grab you a coffee sure Billy, or uh Brian."

That was Jemma. She was an old friend (well acquaintance anyway) of mine. She was a journalist, currently with local radio. She had swapped a shock of purple hair for pink since I'd last seen her and I had swapped names.

"There you go, sorry I haven't got long bud," she said, taking a sip and looking at me over the mug.

We were sitting opposite one other, in a little snug office, more a broom cupboard than anything else. It reminded me of where the presenters used to sit on kids' TV in the eighties.

There was a silence, just verging on an awkward one.

"Look, Jemma, I'm sorry about before. It seems I was pretty confused and…"

"Don't worry about it," she said, raising a hand uncomfortably for me to stop.

"I know, but I remember I was trying to ask you a favour and it didn't really make sense and I've probably a nerve to come here and ask for another one."

"You're after a favour?" she asked, sounding colder than she probably meant to.

"Well, I am, but I've got you a present," I said with my finest attempt at a boyish smile.

"Well, maybe then," she said and let out a little laugh.

She returned my smile, though she still was more standoffish than usual.

Wrinkling her brow, she said, "So, you're Brian now?"

"Yep," I replied simply, shrugging.

"I should have come and visited you," she said quietly.

"No, no, I wasn't so great," I said, waving it away. "I needed time to get myself straight."

"I suppose we all go a bit crazy sometimes," she said, running her hands down her baggy ethnic dress, bangles jingling against it. "Shit," she said suddenly, looking anxious, "I didn't mean…"

"No, I know what you mean," I said, my turn to wave it away. "I was pretty nutty."

We both took a sip of coffee, the tension was cracked a little thank God.

"So, what's this favour?"

"Well, it's just a bit of digging, only if you have time. It's for a case I'm working on. Incidentally, I'm not crazy or anything, this is genuine, I'm well recovered, got the certificates to prove it and everything."

"Okay, okay," she said, giggling into her drink, making a rolling movement with one hand.

"I'm doing a job for a fella name of Hertogen; he has links to the Belgian Embassy. I'm just wanting to see if you can come across anything at all about him, or I suppose anything much about the embassy."

"That sounds doable," she said, crossing her legs on her swivel chair. "What about this pressie then?"

"Aha!" I said, dramatically pulling out a plastic bag. "There you are."

"Thanks, a five-p bag," she said and winked.

I rolled my eyes.

She opened it and looked genuinely pleased.

"Percy French—a collection of songs and poems."

"It's a first edition."

She made an audible guffaw.

"Yeah, I know, I'm a legend! I picked it up in a second-hand shop in Newcastle. I remembered your love of all that shite and thought you'd dig it."

"Aww thank you," she said warmly and put an arm around me. "You've got your favour."

She smelt and felt good.

***

I went along by myself to the gig, originally Tim was going to come with me. The Waterfront is a large, circular affair with glass windows all around. The main hall has a fairly modern interior, primarily built for orchestras. It didn't matter that night, the Blind Boys blew me away. I had been a fan for a few years, since getting into their recent albums, filled full of gospel blues, mean slide, and incredible five-part harmonies. They only won their first Grammy in 2000, after forming in 1939! Yes, they were together almost a quarter of a century before The Beatles had their first hits!

Jimmy Carter on lead vocals sounded as incredible as ever, despite being well into his eighties. He had an easy touch when conversing with the audience too and at one point encouraged fans to buy some merchandise and get it signed afterwards, adding, "If you buy a CD or T-shirt, you'll see a blind boy down at the grocery store tomorrow. Blind Boys gotta eat!" he declared in a southern drawl, tagging on a warm and raspy chortle at the end. I did as he asked and made my way to the stall at the end of the night and joined the queue. Three of the blind members were seated in their golden suits and black sunglasses. My mind went blank and I couldn't think of what to say. No word of a lie, I blurted out what was meant to be an attempt at small talk: "I hope you've enjoyed Belfast. I suppose you haven't got to do much sightseeing," I said. They all looked up for a moment as I cringed and tried to hide my facial expression on instinct. One of them let out a laugh and carried on signing his name.

***

First thing the next day, I rang Hertogen. We agreed to meet that night, for dinner in 'Bert's.' It's a fine dining jazz bar in the five-star Belfast hotel The Merchant. I had a cigarette outside and passed the time with the porter, dressed in full tails and hat. Him, not me. I had made the effort and had a short sleeved, striped shirt on underneath my jacket.

"Mr. Caskey, please take a seat. Have a glass of wine."

I sat down opposite Hertogen, at a table for two, off to the left-hand side at the window.

"Thanks, it's some place this," I said, taking in the deep reds of the plush curtains and the stripes of thick wallpaper. It was Art Deco style, the bar being newly built onto the side of the opulent old bank headquarters. I poured myself a glass of red and topped up his glass too. At the front of the room, there's a low stage and a band were just setting up, piano, double bass, and drums.

"Here you are sir," said a middle-aged waiter, handing me a menu and oozing professionalism from beneath his immaculate crisp suit. "Can I organise you a drink, some mineral water perhaps? For the specials today we have herring and lime soup, Fillet Juan for main, and also there is a very fresh seabass alongside quail eggs on a bed of asparagus risotto."

"Thanks," I said and glanced at Hertogen, hoping for some glimmer of a smile at how fancy the place was. He looked at ease. Just me then.

"I'll take a pint of Guinness for now, thanks," I said.

The waiter grimaced somewhat. "We only sell by the half pint," he said.

"That's fine, bring me two," I replied, smirking.

By the time the main course arrived, the band was in full flow. They seemed decent and were offering some stuff I recognised, middle of the road jazz I supposed.

"You know Brian, I can call you Brian?"

"Please do," I said.

"I am pleased that we can discuss matters together this evening."

"Yeah, I appreciate you paying," I said with a cheeky smile.

"But of course," he said and sounded like Pepé Le Pew to me. I stifled a laugh.

"These guys are pretty good," I offered. "I'm not big into jazz."

He flashed a toothy smile. "I think this not to be jazz," he said.

We both took a sip of our drinks.

"Brian, I am glad you have agreed to stay with the case, I am confident in your abilities and appreciate your discretion."

"What's our guy been up to the last few days? Are you hoping that we can intercept some other messages?"

He sat back in his chair, to the side, raising an eyebrow.

"I did not actually want you to intercept the first message, though I admit it was in fact a bonus. I ask you only to observe and not to get too close. No, I do not want you to intercept anything."

"That's fine," I said evenly, skewering a piece of my medium steak and rubbing it in creamy sauce.

"He has been continuing to make various stops around Belfast, but not making any longer stop offs, nothing again in Bangor or similar to that. I do not think these general visits he makes, concerns my interest in him."

"So, are you gonna tell me what the message was?" I said, fixing him a look.

He let out a half chuckle and pulled at his moustache.

"I think not. As I said last time, there is information I cannot share. I have already divulged more than I would have at first wanted."

"Will we grab a cigarette before desert?" I asked, changing the subject.

"Certainly," he said, dabbing at his beard with the white linen napkin.

"It is really quite uncivilised," he said, as he lit a cigarette outside, with an expensive looking Zippo.

"I know, all these new friggen laws. Bloody Brussels putting us out in the cold! We've put Europe out in the cold now," I said with a wink.

Surprisingly he returned a smile, a genuine, humoured one.

"You know, smoking indoors is actually legal throughout Belgium?"

"I didn't, I'll have to go sometime."

We smoked in silence for a moment, out by the hedgerows beside the footpath. A few others were smoking on the other side, including two big men in suits with even bigger cigars. They'd probably stuck them for fifty quid a pop.

"So, are you going to tell me something about the message, throw me a little bone?" I asked in a lowered voice, persistent if nothing else.

He indulged me with a second smile, his eyes twinkling, perhaps only from the alcohol we had been getting through.

"You are quite unrelenting, I do admire that Mr. Chapman, sorry I mean Caskey," he said, shaking his head.

That seemed odd. Had he said Chapman? That was a little weird. I instinctively felt the outside of my trousers pocket for my meds bottle. I took in a long draw. I suppose he had already admitted to doing a little digging on me. I left it to the side.

"I'll take whatever name you like," I said, trying to keep grounded. "Seeing a bit more of the picture would help my investigations."

He dropped his smoke in the metal box on the wall, picked out another thinly rolled number from his cigarette case, and lit it up.

"I can tell you that we were successful in decoding the message. It gave us some more information regarding the group we have under surveillance. We expect there to be another message soon, perhaps a package this time. I must say again though, we only want you to watch, no approaches."

"Okay," I said.

The dessert was a fine tasting crème brûlée. I suggested an Irish coffee each afterwards and we savoured them before a final cigarette. We spoke nothing more about the case and parted as if business associates, finishing a pleasant work dinner.

I fancied a couple more and sauntered down the few streets leading across the Cathedral Quarter, past Saint Anne's and around the back of City Hall to The Sunflower Bar. I took out my top button and gave myself a shake. The slightly 'tumbling in' nature of its exterior greeted me pleasantly, along with the only metal security cage leftover from The Troubles.

As I opened the door, I could hear Trad music being played somewhere inside, hovering over the roar of the packed pub. I got my drink and went on past the players in the corner, harp, guitar, and violin. The Sunflower is one of many pubs to now make the most of their beer gardens for the remaining, hardened smokers. All of the tables in the medium sized garden were taken. I crossed to beyond the outside bar and claimed a piece of wall to lean against. I stayed about an hour, smoked a few cigs. I had a few whiskeys and somewhat sullied them with lemonade and ice. I wasn't in the mood for drinking them straight. I was getting my coat on to leave the beer garden when I felt a hand on my shoulder.

"Billy," the voice said loudly.

I turned around and it took me a moment to place him.

"Glenn, how are you doing?" I said, shaking the stocky and now quite overweight man's hand. He had cut his hair shorter too, looked like it was receding.

"I thought it was you," he said, talking a little like a washing machine.

Glenn had been in the force with me. He was a bit older than me and we had never been mates, mostly because he was a dickhead.

"How's things?" I said, feeling the need to make some small talk.

"Not bad, not bad. I got out a couple of years back, in security now."

I nodded, feigning some interest. He glanced back at his group, and took a drag on his smoke.

"I hear you changed your name," he said, with a twitch in his eye.

"Yeah I did," I said, trying not to come across too sheepish. "It's Brian now."

"Oh," he said, "that's a bit random."

"Well," I replied, "there you are."

"I suppose it's part of being a bigshot writer?" he said, trying to hide the mean spiritedness behind it.

"Fuck off," I said simply and left.

***

When I got home, I fired up the laptop, but creativity wasn't striking. I went through some emails, I'd been putting some things off. There were a couple of interviews for 'blog tours' that I was meant to be sending back to folk. 'Blog Tours?' Me, a virtual, touring author. It was a bit mad. I started to answer the questions, quite enjoying myself. I went to bed thinking I'd come off with more winning quips than Winston Churchill. When I came back to it in the cold light of day I was sober and it was ugly.

Chapter Twenty-Eight

The memories had flooded back in an instant and I tried not to let them in for the moment. It was like my body sweating when it needed to cool down. It was instinctive. I tried to appear nonchalant, but judging by Fotheringay's perplexed impression, not doing a great job of it.

"Sorry, it's just I am an admirer of his work, I hadn't realised it was from his collection," I said hastily.

"Yes, yes I see. An underrated talent, French. But," he added with apparent authority, "one whose credentials as a watercolour artist are certainly on the rise."

We both took a drink and I gathered my thoughts.

"Tell me about the robbery," I said.

"Yes of course," he replied austerely, crossing his legs and stubbing out another fat brown cigar end with a flume of dying smoke. "But there will be plenty of time for all of that. I will take you through exactly what happened tomorrow, step by step in the room where the gallery was on display. First, I want to explain what it is we would like you to concentrate your investigation on, or more plainly, who."

Chapter Twenty-Nine

Mallusk, Newtonabbey, The Falls, one other stop out towards Holywood. Regan wasn't making any longer stops on my first three days, me back on his tail. Hertogen had said the nights were now covered full time by some unspecified person, so just doing the days suited me fine. I kept my distance and Regan gave no sign of noticing me or even looking out for anyone. Each day I clocked off about five or six, once he was home and seemingly going in for his dinner. I waited around a few times to see if I could spot the anonymous colleague of mine, but I didn't. Perhaps they had some CCTV, or bugs maybe. Could be there was someone in one of the houses in his street that was watching. There was no way of me knowing how big this thing could be.

After Regan made a few stops on the Thursday, I followed him, two cars behind, as he made his way along the Westlink. I eased back into the chair, gearing up into fifth. It was an easy gig really. I was happy enough to continue with what I was doing. My duties were clear and I admit I was kind of enjoying letting the mystery unfold itself just as what I was meant to be: an observer. I was satisfied to an extent that I wouldn't get anything more out of Hertogen, until I discovered something further to give to him. I just had to be patient.

As we fed onto the Sydenham Bypass, my mind flitted to Billy Chapman and I tried to work out that mystery a little more too. I know writers are all different, and it's a cliché, but I certainly never know where the story is headed. It's a funny thing. What sort of a man was Gallagher? I wasn't sure. Fotheringay? Dunno. Where did I get that name from? Ahh—The Prisoner. There was a brief character in the 60s show called Fotheringay, must have been from there. Percy French popping up—well I knew where that had come from. What about Billy? What was going on in his head? He was doing okay, enjoying a new case himself. My own 'Hound of Ulster.' Could be a title maybe? Yeah, not bad.

The Hound of Ulster
– Sequel to the bestselling The Chaser on the Rocks.

Ha! Bestselling? I grinned and lit up a smoke. Not exactly a bestseller—I had sold sixty or seventy anyway, last time I checked. Amazon makes you wait two months to see how you're doing. I obsessively checked my ranking, anyway, every couple of hours, driving myself nuts wondering what the algorithms meant. Feckin' Amazon! Up a hundred and fifty, then down three hundred—it would drive you to drink or drugs. I already needed both.

As we came through Holywood, I turned up *Amorica* by The Black Crowes on my stereo and tapped the steering wheel to the Latino beats at the start of *High Head Blues*. I stopped myself belting along to "A charmed life it is, at least they tell you so," as Regan indicated left, heading through Cultra. I switched it off, saying, "Sorry guys." Regan turned off on the flyover to The Ulster Folk and Transport Museum and I followed, luckily one car turning off also, in between us.

I had only ever known one person to live in Cultra. That's because it's usually a pretty bloody snobby spot. It was Jim McAllister, an RUC officer I had worked alongside. He had only afforded a house there because his wife was from a wealthy family. He certainly didn't get it on his constable salary. One night there was a knock on his door and that was it; he was shot dead right there, in front of his wife and kids. That was during a time when there was a supposed 'Ceasefire.'

Regan parked up at the top carpark on the Folk Park end, and I pulled up onto the grassy verge just below it. I watched him walk up to the portacabin kiosk and buy a ticket. The Ulster Folk and Transport museum is essentially 'what it says on the tin.' On the far side, there are two giant buildings, housing historical trains, buses, aeroplanes. There's an original Delorean in there, which, next to hundred-and-fifty-year-old trains, takes you somewhat 'back to the future.' Boom, boom. On the folk side there have been buildings, some hundreds of years old, taken up brick by brick and rebuilt into a village and surrounding farmland. There's churches, a police station, farm houses, dozens of them. The centre has an early twentieth century style square and even has a pub. Unfortunately, they don't serve any drink in it.

I waited for Regan to turn up the path towards the start of the folk park, and I followed at distance and then bought a ticket too. It cost me the guts of a tenner and I made a mental note to be sure to claim it on expenses. I paused as a family of four with a stroller and a pram made their way up in front of me, and I could make out Regan, turning the corner up ahead past the sweet shop and blacksmith's. I lit a cigarette and made my way up the cobbled street, passing an Orange Lodge, now the visitor centre.

I took out my map and pretended to inspect it. I hadn't been there in years, but had gone plenty of times as a kid and didn't need it. I walked on, passing a few more groups of tourists. I got to the top of the hill, next to the coal merchant and saw Regan crossing across the green. I stopped and watched, peering over my map. A couple with a toddler rushed past me, almost dragging the child as it yelled, while skilfully keeping a dummy in her mouth.

Regan stopped by a bin and stubbed out a cigarette on the metal lid. He looked around quickly and then walked on. He crossed in front of the café, past the photographer's and into the old picture house. I walked over to the tables outside the café and took a seat. It was chilly enough out and the only customers were a few families, seated inside. I zipped up my jacket and lit another smoke. I positioned myself side on to the cinema and kept it in peripheral vision, as I surveyed the square. A few more families passed on by and a museum volunteer in full, maybe, 1920s RUC uniform. I enjoyed the cigarette and was enjoying the chase too. I eyed everyone who passed, no obvious contenders for a contact. I supposed there'd be some kind of gap though anyway, between the two, or it would hardly be worth the trouble. That was if there was any message at all. My phone started to buzz in my pocket.

"Hello?"

"Bil... Brian how you doing?"

"Oh hi Jemma, how's it going?"

"Dead on, look, I just wanted to ring you quickly. I'm afraid I couldn't turn up anything on your Hertogen character. In fact nothing at all, buddy."

"Oh, okay, don't worry. Thanks for trying," I said, expecting as much.

"That's all right. I looked into the embassy too, not much of interest that I could see. It's actually a consulate just—up around Gilnahirk. It's a wee small office and just does the day to day stuff for Belgian nationals."

"Okay, cheers for looking anyway," I said, distracted.

"If you want to give me any more information?"

"No, no that's okay, but thanks Jemma."

"All right then, I'd better run," she said, less chirpy.

"Okay... here, I owe you a coffee."

"Okay hon," she said and hung up.

Fair enough. I hadn't really anticipated much different. I didn't think Hertogen would be his real name either.

After another five minutes, Regan emerged. He stopped at the door and looked around again, lighting up a new cigarette. He walked behind me, crossed the green, and returned back towards the first street, Tea Lane. I stood up and made as if I was heading to the church, walking past the post office and bank. I watched discreetly as Regan walked down the road and to the entrance path. I crossed to beside the church, from where you can see the carpark, through the trees on the mossy bank. He headed on out to his car, got in, and took off. I waited a second until he was definitely away and then crossed back across the green.

The square was quiet and nobody else was heading towards the cinema. I approached the old whitewashed building, which looked more like a church hall. I stepped inside to the entrance hall, where there was a table and chairs set for tea, and a small staircase leading up to a projectionist's booth. There was a rail sectioning if off at the top, but you could look into the room, all set up with period equipment. I walked on past, through the faded red curtains and into the blacked out main hall. It was filled with rows of old, scored pews and on creaky wooden floor boards. The walls were stone and cold. All was partially lit by the light from the screen and a jittery, washed out projection on the back wall. The film was the original German Expressionist version of Nosferatu. It was just coming to the bit where the creepy stagecoach driver arrives and leads the protagonist up the mountain to the vampire's castle.

I glanced back to the door and then began my search. I guessed there might be another sheet hidden or even something smaller, maybe a memory stick. Of course there still mightn't have been anything to find at all. Whatever may have been left, it could have been hidden anywhere. I checked along all the pews, against the walls, on the small stage, and I very thoroughly searched the rickety piano off to the side. I returned to the hall and checked through the drawers of an old dresser, on the table, even in the teapot. Nothing. I looked back towards the red curtain and thought maybe I should try back in the hall again. I looked up at the short staircase and the projectionist's room, cordoned off with a rope. Would Regan chance getting caught in there? Maybe.

I quickly walked up the steps and stood up against the rope, peering in. The room was dominated by an old grey projector. It was lit up, but I figured the movie was really running off a DVD. There was a tiny bit of floor space on the far side of the rope and a little chest and a table, with various period objects scattered about. Fuck it. I lifted a leg over the rope. Crack! The door below shot open beneath me and I jolted and awkwardly swivelled my leg back around. There was the shuffle of feet and I stood still, looking innocuously into the projector room, like just another tourist.

"C'mon Evie," said a young mother, manoeuvring a pram through the narrow entrance. I turned and offered a friendly look.

"Can I give you a hand?" I shouted down.

"I'm okay thanks," replied the harassed looking mother. A toddler ran in behind her, holding onto a museum map in one hand, and tighter still, to a packet of chocolate buttons in the other.

I exhaled heavily.

"Look, it's a cinema from the olden days," said the mother, feigning enthusiasm. "Come over and see."

She pushed the pram on towards the curtain and the toddler came up behind her,

"Where are the snacks?" she asked.

"No sweetheart, there's no snacks."

"I'm hungry."

"We'll get something soon, come over and see."

They went in through the curtains and I heard them shuffle on in. I came down the steps and pretended to read the information board, with an old cut out photograph of the original picture house. The baby started a low cry that rapidly turned into a roar, maybe she was hungry too. The curtain parted again. The mother swivelled the pram around, a new couple of lines on her forehead.

"Right, let's have a look in the farmhouse, they're baking some soda, then we'll go for a snack."

They traipsed back across the hall and I walked over and held the door for them.

"Thanks," said the weary mother.

"Cheerio," I said, closing the door behind them.

Sitting down at the table, I breathed out again, this time loudly.

"Fuck," I said quietly to myself.

I got up, jogged up the steps, and climbed straight over the rope. I hastily riffled through the few drawers; nothing... nothing... nothing... bingo! There was a brown envelope in the bottom drawer of the desk. It looked promising. I crossed back to the door and glanced down, and then ducked back inside. I carefully emptied the contents onto the desk. There was a passport, British, recently issued. I opened it out and a youngish black face with a beard and short hair looked back at me. He was Lee Blakey, apparently. There was a sheet too. It was an internet flight printout, one seat booked for a guy with the same name. It was for the next week, a one-way ticket to Charleroi, Brussels.

Chapter Thirty

I took breakfast at a small table, alone, the next morning. The pot of coffee, following a good fry up, helped focus my attention, my brain still paddling in a pool of alcohol. I lit a cigarette, but it tasted foul and I stubbed it out. I looked out the window and told my brain it was time to get a towel.

Terry Gallagher. That was the name of my quarry. Fotheringay had laid out why he was the prime target of suspicion. Gallagher was the brother-in-law of McBride and that was the reason for their not wanting a police investigation. Apparently, ever since McBride's sister had died from polio a few years before, he had gone somewhat off the rails and developed some money problems too. He worked at the Donard as a waiter and had been missing since the night of the theft. Nobody had any idea where he was.

After I was sufficiently breakfasted, I crossed to the Leopold function room (the Belgian had enjoyed the hospitality of several Irish hotels it seemed) and knocked on the large double doors. After a few seconds, Fotheringay answered, his moustache crinkling into a half smile.

"Old chap, come on through. How's the head?"

"Fine, just fine," I lied. The night before ostensibly had washed easily off the other man.

I walked on through, finding myself in a medium sized ballroom. It had been emptied of its chairs, revealing a recently polished parquet floor. The walls were papered in a rich royal blue and up above them was ornate cornicing. I took out my lighter and started to click it. There were only the two of us in the room and

Fotheringay's voice echoed deeply, like the Lord's Prayer spoken by a congregation in an old chapel.

"Isn't it splendid?" he asked crisply. "Fine plaster work, outstanding."

"It is. Impressive," I said, perhaps showing more interest in my petrol lighter that wouldn't spark the flint. It eventually took and I inhaled and had another look around. There were large windows on one side, with only a small opening latch in each, near the high ceiling. There were a few vents in the walls and a couple of plaques and some hooks where paintings had been hung. Apart from that, the walls were bare.

"Whereabouts were the paintings hung?" I asked.

He talked me through how the exhibition had been set out, where the paintings were placed, and where the staff members were working, who had seen what and so forth. Unfortunately, there wasn't much to tell. I scratched at my neck. My head hurt. At least I was getting paid something either way.

"How does the hotel feel about all of this? Not involving the police, for instance?"

"Well, they have been most cooperative," he said, pausing. "Mr. McBride is very well thought of, and you could say... influential. There is also the matter of one of their staff being involved. They are happy to let us carry out our little investigation and have placed themselves at our disposal."

I shrugged and blew out some smoke. The back door blew ajar and the draft pricked my back.

"Where does that lead to?"

"Oh, there is a short, windowless corridor that leads back to the kitchens. We suspect that the paintings were taken out that way. After the exhibition was completed and the room had been serviced, it was locked from both ends. This was around one a.m. and the room was opened again at nine thirty the next morning, to begin the set up for

another function. That is when I had arrived with some of my staff to remove the paintings, and we discovered it had been ransacked. The room had been locked from both ends."

"Yeah, you said that, okay," I said thinking and looking for somewhere to stick my cig end. I settled on a dish that held a large candle on the huge granite fireplace. "So why in particular do you figure Mr. McBride's brother-in-law?"

He carefully clipped a fat cigar with a circular cutter and threw the end on the floor, before swiftly striking a match. He puffed two or three times and raised an eyebrow, indicating for me to wait a moment.

"Firstly, there is the matter of his recent erratic behaviour. Secondly, there are his money problems. Thirdly, all internal bunches of keys have been accounted for except the set belonging to Mr. Gallagher. Then of course, we also have his disappearance. It does not look good I am afraid."

"Okay, but it could still have been somebody else. They could have done the job and replaced the keys. Or, someone could have taken a set and then replaced them."

He took a few more puffs and exhaled a plume of brown smoke.

"Yes, perhaps," he said somewhat dismissively, "that is possible. We of course welcome your full investigation, but I feel he is the only real suspect."

I stared out the window at the sweeping driveway, lined by evergreens and lampposts, and then returned my gaze to Fotheringay,

"There is also the question of where Mr. Gallagher is. It is surely possible that he has been hurt or become involved in some other way, I mean, against his will."

"I think that unlikely," he replied crisply.

Chapter Thirty-One

When I was back in the car, I checked the photo on my phone. The passport looked dead on. I swiped the screen and you could read the printout just about too. Good. I had placed everything back where I had found them in the projectionist's booth and had an uneventful walk back to my car. Thank fuck. What had I got mixed up in? I really was frigged to try and work it out. I had no clue. A Belgian diplomat. Secret messages. A local gang that had something to do with my dead wristband guy. And now, secret papers to get some fella to Belgium? I needed a drink.

***

Horatio Todds was quiet. It was still only the afternoon, after all. Todds has become a popular local in East Belfast, for those not wanting to drink in a paramilitary dive. These days, that counted for quite a few. I had a booth to myself and took a pint of Guinness. If it went down well, I figured I'd leave the car, have a few more, and walk back home. The waitress who had served me walked past, collecting glasses. She gave a sweet smile as she walked by. She looked like your average girl next door, but a girl next door who you really fancied. "Easy Caskey," I said to myself. Jesus, I'd be old enough to be her drunk uncle. A local band's underground anthem of 'Get her home, get her bucked,' intruded into my head and I stifled a laugh. I of course did neither. I shook my head and settled myself.

Sipping through the head of my stout, I fiddled with my phone. I was due a call from Hertogen for a general update. He'd be getting more than was expected. It was bloody annoying that he didn't give me a number that I could get him on. As I was dwelling on this, almost immediately the phone rang.

"Hello, is that Brian?"

I was thrown by a limey accent and hadn't checked who was calling, presuming it was Hertogen.

"Yeah, who's this?" I asked, a bit abruptly.

"Oh, I'm sorry, this is Doctor Vine."

Of course, that's who owned the voice, it was my doctor, my psychiatrist. Shit, I thought, had I missed an appointment?

"You missed an appointment Brian." Oh yes then, shit. "I just wanted to check that you were all right," he continued.

"Yes, yes I'm fine, look shit, I mean, sorry, it just slipped my mind."

Dr. Vine had been decent to me, a change from some of the fuckwits I had seen previously. He was an Englishman, mid-forties, dead on for a quack.

"That's all right, it's just that our little meetings are important, you know, we wouldn't want things to slip."

"No, it's nothing like that, I've been distracted with writing and some new work, but I'll ring into your office tomorrow and get something rescheduled, sorry about that."

"That's grand Brian, I'll look forward to that. I hope you are not taking on too much, we've discussed before how that can affect you."

"No, no I'm being careful, I'm enjoying my work. See you soon Doctor."

"Take care Billy."

I hung up and sank the remainder of my pint. I reached into my pocket and took out my pills. Did he say Billy? He never was keen on me changing my name, anyway. Had I taken one earlier? I took two, just to be on the safe side.

There was a message waiting on my phone from an unknown number. I presumed it was Hertogen. Probably on a burner. It read simply, "I will ring you again shortly for an update."

I wrote back, "I have just found something new that will interest you."

A reply came after a few seconds. "I will send a car to your house at 8 p.m. instead."

Chapter Thirty-Two

I spent the afternoon tracking down friends and associates of Gallagher. There were work colleagues from the hotel, a cousin, a former landlady, and his neighbours. This took most of the day and I only paused for a few coffees along the way, no proper drinks. I didn't have far to travel, Newcastle is a small town and I was able to get back and forth, only covering a few miles by the end of it. I sat with a last coffee before the proper drinks, about six that evening, on a scarlet sofa in the hotel lobby. I took my time over a cigarette, examining its burning tip every couple of seconds, deep in thought. All I had discovered so far was that Gallagher was a decent sort of fella, though still cut up over his wife's death. He seemingly kept to himself for a large part, but there was no mention of any erratic behaviour, even when I suggested it to folk. There was also no mention from anyone of any money concerns. It would appear he had gained a small inheritance from his wife's family's wealth and was comfortable. He appeared to be well thought of in his job too.

"Mr. Chapman, there is a telephone call for you at reception," a bus boy in oversized outfit informed me.

I looked up, still lost in my thoughts. "Okay, thanks, I'll be right there."

I gathered myself and followed him over to the side of the large reception desk.

"Chapman here."

"Mr. Chapman, this is Fotheringay."

"Hello Mr. Fotheringay, how can I help you?"

"I wanted to inform you that Mr. McBride will be arriving on the train first thing tomorrow and we would like to meet with you in the morning."

"Yes, sure, that's grand. Am I in trouble with the headmaster?" I asked, chewing my lip.

"No, not at all," he said with a jarring laugh. "He would just like to discuss the progress of the case thus far."

"Fine, I'll see you then."

"Thank you," he said eagerly. "And you will be dining in the restaurant tonight?"

"Yes, I reckon so."

"Good, good, I can recommend the salmon, everything paid for on me of course. I must go now, enjoy your evening."

"Thank you," I said, before hanging up. I don't like salmon much and I wasn't sure about Fotheringay.

Chapter Thirty-Three

I tilted open my living room blinds at five to eight. There was a black BMW waiting outside with official plates. I locked up promptly and went on out. I didn't bother trying to make conversation with the suited driver of the plush Beamer. He only spoke to tell me that he was taking me to see Hertogen, and once again when we stopped at the Europa Hotel, he said to go to room 141. His accent was some kind of European, probably one of the ones lucky to still be in the EU, I didn't know which.

I walked on into the lobby of the glass fronted five-star hotel. It's a very trendy, but also sumptuous kind of place. When the MTV awards were in town a few years ago, all the big celebs stayed there. It sits opposite the infamous Crown Bar, but is infamous itself for the questionable honour of being the most bombed hotel in the world, after thirty-six attacks by the IRA. Well, those days are gone, hopefully.

I knocked twice on room 141, and after a moment Hertogen answered. He led me inside to a plush executive suite, with plenty of room for a table and chairs out by themselves, approximately three miles from the bed. On the table was a bottle of Sauvignon Blanc in a cooler and two glasses. One was already half empty. Maybe half full—but that's just me.

"Can I offer you a drink?"

"Thank you, as always, I will accept," I said and we both sat.

Hertogen gave me a somewhat uneasy smile; he didn't like being in the position of not knowing something that someone else did. Maybe he just didn't like 'me' knowing something he didn't.

"Well?" he said slowly, after swilling some wine around in his mouth. "What is it you have to report?"

"I'll get straight to it. Regan stopped off at another museum today—The Folk Park in Cultra—you know of it?"

"I am afraid not," he said, refilling his glass.

"Okay, well, it's laid out with a load of old buildings, not that many people about it, out of season. I know you said to make no advances and I didn't exactly, but I did find something. Pretty important, I would reckon actually."

I plucked out my phone and scrolled through to my photos.

"I found these. Have a flick through. If you see pictures of me in the buff, you've gone too far."

He accepted the phone with a sardonic curl of the lip. He slowly swiped a finger over the screen, expressionless. Setting the phone down again after a moment, he placed his hands on his folded knees and glanced up at the ceiling, before setting his eyes on me, purposefully.

"Mr. Caskey, I trust you did not disturb the items?" he asked, strained.

"Nope, set them back where I found them and there was nobody else suspicious nearby either. Nobody saw me."

"And there was definitely nothing else hidden?"

"No, not that I could find, and I looked pretty hard. So, do you know this guy?"

A flicker of irritation crossed his face; I think I interrupted his trail of thought.

"Yes, but not under that name. Mr. Chapman, please send me those photographs and then delete them from your phone."

"Okay, but I'm gonna need more information if I'm to carry on with this thing."

He blew out air and scratched his knee, looking away.

"It is the right time to allow me to take you into my confidence further," he said quietly.

I did as he asked as nonchalantly as I could, eager to not appear eager.

"There you are," I said and passed him my phone.

He checked it briefly and took out his own. He typed at it for a second and set it down again, picking up my own again.

"I need to delete your sent items and history."

"That's fine," I said and watched him typing at my phone, it making me a little uncomfortable. "I haven't saved it to my computer or anything," I offered.

"I would trust not," he said, distracted.

"There," he said, handing me it back. "This is one of the few smoking rooms, please feel free."

"Cheers, I will," I said, rustling eagerly through my pockets, noticing that my palms were sweaty.

He lit a thinly made roll up and placed his lighter beside the glass ashtray. It still shone in places, except where a few new butts lay that had been stubbed out on the rim.

"If I am to provide you with further confidential information, I need your agreement that you would be willing to carry out further surveillance, which... might involve more of your time and some travelling."

"You mean like to Brussels?"

"Perhaps, would you be open to this?"

It would have been stupid for me to continue on with the case, with one thing and another, mostly my mental health. Really stupid.

"What would the terms be?" I asked.

"It would still be just for surveillance, maybe even to be only 'on call' in a location to carry this out, maybe you wouldn't be called on while there at all."

"And the payment?"

"You would receive double what you get a day now, plus expenses."

I finished my smoke and found I was nodding. I stopped it. I tried to look thoughtful and unconvinced.

"That may be agreeable, but you need to be straighter with me."

"Fine. Then we are agreed."

I took a sip noncommittally and waited for him to continue.

"Regan and the group he is a part of are involved in a wide range of criminal activities. Some of these have overlapped with the gang that your young thief worked with. The man in this photograph is another link along in the chain. More accurately, he is many links higher."

"So you've been trailing some regular criminals to get you information on much more, how would say, important parties?"

"Exactly," he said, like a pleased headmaster. "Intelligence had suggested to us that there was already a possible link between these two groups. The man in the photograph is of interest to many. He is not a wanted man as such, but very much a person of interest, shall we say. And when I say that others are interested, I am speaking of important people. I am talking about people who work for places, work for countries and agencies that like using single letters and numbers as their names."

"Okay, I get it. What do they want him for?"

"I will tell you this last thing only. He is most likely involved with those who plan terror attacks."

He stopped and gauged my reaction. I felt calm. I had an inkling that it could be something like that, but had thought I was maybe getting carried away.

"He has very credible links to several cells," he continued. "One of these we have identified and have placed an agent insider with it, in Brussels."

I lit up a new cigarette and felt a nice little buzz on.

"Okay," I said with a grin, "I love sprouts—and waffles."

Chapter Thirty-Four

I had just ordered my desert and Irish coffee with pouring cream, when the first shot rang out. I was up on my feet, there was a communal gasp and someone dropped some cutlery. Then the second shot followed.

Chapter Thirty-Five

Buzzo reminded me that I had missed a feed. It was when he flicked my lighter off the top of the bed that I got up, surviving the previous few missiles he had sent my way. I felt in quite the daze, but two cups of coffee and walking through my WRAP made me feel pretty okay. I got a wriggle on. I was in Tim's room, having a third cup, by eleven.

"Are you doing any better?" I asked him, knowing the answer wouldn't be that positive, noting the greying of his skin and some visible weight loss.

"Not great really, Brian, I'm sick of talking about it to be honest, but hey, how have you been doing—both jobs?" he asked, managing to sound fairly enthusiastic.

"Yeah it's okay, the book's selling a wee bit and well, this new job I've got on, is pretty intense."

"Really?" he asked with concern. "Hope you're not taking on too much."

I decided to continue on. If he didn't want to talk about his illness, I wasn't going to make him.

"No, everyone keeps asking me that, but it's grand. It's nothing I can't handle. I can't say too much—you know the score—but it's an interesting one—might need to do a spot of travel too."

"Well, good," he replied, sitting up a little. "I'm happy for you, just go easy." He shot me a look. "You didn't bring me another wee drink by any chance?"

"Yeah, I might have something," I said evenly.

"Good, cheers," he said, his eyes sparkling with a touch more life about them. "So what about them Glens on Saturday? Fucking appalling."

"You and me could do a better job, even the state we're in," I agreed.

***

I popped into the Linen Hall library afterwards for a wee look around. I had done a reading there a few months before and I had never had a proper look about. It's a traditional old place and I spent a pleasant half hour exploring around it. There was something I had wanted to do for a while and I worked myself up to it, lifting out my library card as I headed to the main desk. I wanted my 'J.R. Hartley moment.'

"Hello, I'd like to reserve a book please."

"Certainly," said the lady in the yellow jumper and glasses, disinterestedly. "Your card please."

I pushed it across and she started to plug in the numbers.

"What is the title you're after?"

"A Chaser on the Rocks," I said, a flutter in my stomach.

"Chaser, chaser," she said, scrolling down her screen. "Who's the author?" she asked, squinting a little.

"Oh, it's Brian Caskey."

She typed it in.

"Nothing I'm afraid. We mustn't have it or be ordering that one I'm afraid."

She glanced at my card and then back at the screen.

"Oh," she said, "is this you?"

"Yes, don't worry," I said hurriedly, wishing I had rejected this little exercise.

She offered a sympathetic smile. I rushed onwards, leaving a small part of my soul on the floor.

My next stop was the Ulster Museum. I hadn't visited since I was researching my first novel and I wanted to fact check a few things for the new one. I jogged up Botanic Gardens, after parking near the university when a light rain started. I don't generally jog. The familiar shape of the museum greeted me out of the undergrowth, looking like a huge artillery bunker that someone had misplaced. I headed for the café first as always and enjoyed a caramel square and a cappuccino. I then set about with my notebook, jotting down some bits and bobs over the course of an hour or so. There was a new exhibition on the Easter Rising of 1916. Nothing to do with what I was writing, but interesting none the less. I may be an old prod from East Belfast, but I'm pretty open minded these days, quite the modern man.

***

I went back to the office for the afternoon, in case any other international men of mystery wanted me for anything. Hertogen was due to ring, once he had found out some more information and had decided on what he wanted me to do. I was lighting up a cigarette when the mobile made me jump out of my chair. I instinctively made a 'playing it cool' face, though nobody was there to see it. I looked at the screen—Mary calling.

"Hello?"

"Hello Billy, or sorry, Brian, how are you?"

"Yeah, I'm good, how are you?"

"I'm grand. Hey, look, I just wanted to see how you're doing, hadn't heard from you since the book launch."

"Yeah, sorry, I've been up to my eyes. Things good yourself?"

"Yeah, just work busy as usual, same old shit. I just wanted to… you know, check in."

"I'm always glad to hear from you Mary," I said, pausing. "I'm really okay, you don't need to be worrying about me."

"Well, I do," she said somewhat abruptly. "I'm glad you're all right. Will we grab a coffee sometime?"

"Yeah, sounds good. The only thing is I might be going away for a few days."

"Oh, really?" she replied dubiously.

"It's a case, might need to be away a couple of nights soon."

"Billy, do you think that's wise?" she said, her voice doused with some liquid nitrogen.

"Mary, I appreciate your concern, but I'm a big boy."

"Brian, it wasn't long ago that, well, you know all that happened..."

"Yes I do," I cut in. "Things are fine, I know what I'm doing."

"I hope so. Well, I still don't think it's a good idea."

I was getting irritated.

"I'm sorry you don't, but we're not married anymore, so..."

"Right fine, do what you want!" she said losing her temper.

Silence.

"I better go, I'm in work, see you soon," she said quietly and cut the line.

Fucksake.

I reached for my smokes and lit one. The phone rang again.

"Hello," I answered gruffly.

"Brian? Can you talk? I have a secure line."

Hertogen, right, go on then, I thought.

I listened, trying to both concentrate and to settle myself.

"Okay, yes I'll do it," I said at the end.

It was too late now.

***

I stopped off at the Great Eastern on the way home and ordered a Guinness. It was quiet and I took a booth in the corner to myself. There were a few faces I recognised and I received a couple of nods and returned them, I just didn't chat to anyone. Well, just the barman, who I ordered a second pint off after a bit and a plate of chips for my dinner. I played about on my phone and half paid attention to an episode of 'Pointless' on the TV set on the wall. I felt nervous, but not so much that I wanted to back off from it all. I had been pushing myself for a while. I had got over my big health dip. I had got a novel published. And, I was starting cases again, and I was still in control. I suppose it's like the kind of nervousness I got when I used to play amateur league football. I knew I'd be wrecked and probably get a bit of a hiding, but I still wanted to do it.

"Heart of the Matter, The Third Man, Honourable Consul," I mouthed to myself.

The final round of 'Pointless' asked for the least known Graham Greene novels. I watched on, they went for The Third Man and two others I didn't know. They won! I waited for the list after—I love it when I get a pointless one. Shite—none of them. Flip—I hadn't realised how well known his books still were. Oh well. I went home, feeling happy enough with my lot. Though as Mr. Greene said, "Point me out the happy man and I will point you out either egotism, selfishness, evil—or else an absolute ignorance." I probably could have ticked quite a few of those boxes.

Chapter Thirty-Six

*M*ost *got to their feet but no farther. I ran through the dining room and towards where the gunfire had come from. Out in the hall, a few waitresses were letting out shrieks and waiters were standing still with their arms the same length, not feeling like being heroes. Some had started to gather around the Leopold room where I presumed the noise had come from. The tall, middle aged maitre d' started to hammer on the door and call into the room, but no more noise came from inside. The hotel manager, Mr. Parsons, ran past me, a stout, balding man with glasses. He managed to give me a nod as he passed, I had met him briefly the previously day. I jogged on with him as he fumbled for his keys. The maitre d' continued to hammer on the door. The key was put in, turned, and we all waited for a second.*

"Let me go in first if you like," I said.

The manager gave me a reluctant nod and pulled the door ajar. I slipped in and the others followed close behind, the assorted staff flapping out in the hall behind us. There was one standard light illuminating the room from out of the darkness. There was a single chair in front of the fireplace and a body on the floor beside it. The blood looked black, oozing out from underneath the body. I walked over towards the corpse and the other two hung back. It was a man, in perhaps his late forties, with a gaping hole in his side. A few feet from the chair lay a 45 Browning M1911. I walked on past and looked about the empty room. It was bare and still, and cold. I crossed to the back door and tried the handle. It was locked. I gave a start when a knocking and shouting began abruptly from the other side. It must have been the kitchen staff, I thought. I turned back, the other two were issuing instructions to their staff out in the hall, and then they closed the door. I walked swiftly towards them, crossing past the body.

"He's dead. I warn you, it's not pretty," I said urgently.

They looked at one another nervously and then at me. I walked back to the centre of the room and they followed me, a few steps behind, used to being of service, but not subservient. I stopped at the man's feet and they came up beside him.

"Do you know him?"

They looked at each other again and then at me.

"That's Gallagher," said Parsons.

"Poor bastard," agreed the maitre d'.

Chapter Thirty-Seven

Ryanair isn't known for its frills. The plane had seats and also a metal shell, protecting me from the clouds and a large drop. That was about it. I had to go from Aldergrove, which is not as close as the City Airport, *George Best City* that is. It's a few miles drive and costs a mortgage to park at, but hey. I was looking forward to it being *Brian Caskey Airport* one day. There'd probably be a better chance of it being called *Gerry Adams Airport* before that.

I sank a pint in the bar beforehand, after the most expensive 'Ulster' I had ever consumed and certainly not the best. In saying that, a fry and a pint at five in the morning is quite the novelty—well for most of us anyway. As we flew over the choppy Irish Sea, it reminded me how small Northern Ireland is, especially considering the amount of trouble it's caused. Countries, kingdoms, counties, provinces—it's had all sorts and who knows what in the future! The legend says that the way Ulster was won in the first place is a pretty gruesome tale. Also, apparently it's the reason for the 'Red Hand of Ulster' emblem, that is popular with various loyalist paramilitaries. The story goes that there was a boat race between noblemen and the first to touch land would be crowned King of Ulster. When one man was lagging behind and seemed destined to lose, he chopped off his own hand and threw it onto the shore. Seemed a bit drastic to me!

I was enjoying a follow up Bush and ice when the pilot told us to put our seatbelts back on and that the no smoking sign was back on, frig knows why, when you couldn't smoke on a plane for years. It made me itch even more to be back on land. I filled my lungs once I had collected my bags and was out on the street beside

Charleroi Airport. I felt good. Not just to smoke, good all around.

One thing though, it was pretty cold. April in Belgium apparently is. I pulled my jacket closer and slung my bag off my shoulder and onto the ground. I looked around at mostly suits and students ambling around, all in a hurry. Hertogen had already advised me on the transport arrangements and my tickets were all paid for.

I put my smoke out responsibly in a metal box provided and joined the queue for the bus terminal. The airport was reasonably large, bigger than I'd been to in years anyway. I enjoyed hearing the foreign accents and recognised a smattering of French here and there. Another language I heard, but didn't know, was I guessed probably Flemish.

Brussels is a divided city in many ways, through two distinct cultures and identities. So my guidebook told me anyway. They didn't tend to shoot and bomb each other though. It was cold, but not the same as home. I began to slowly move up the queue and flicked through Facebook and BBC News, getting a good enough signal on it. I slipped it back in my pocket after a few minutes and thought about my writing. What next for *The Hound*? Could I get him to travel to Brussels too? Look up some distant descendant of Leopold? I thought not.

After nearly an hour of waiting about, I filed onto the bus and managed to scavenge a window seat. Many more commuters packed on behind me. I heaved my bag up onto the rack and sat back down again. I had planned on taking in the sights on the thirty-mile drive to Brussels, but I was asleep before the first five.

***

I came to, with a start, to the rustling of bags and the sensation of bodies moving around me. I rubbed at my eyes. Half the bus had already emptied and I shot up and instinctively pulled down my bag. I felt lightheaded and sat down again for a moment. I righted myself and got up and off the bus.

Brussels Central is a hectic station, more pickpockets than passengers, so they say. I put on my old RUC face and held my wallet tight to my ribs in my inside pocket. Let's face it, I was never much of a cop, but I could at least make the face. I took it out again when I was in a bit of space outside and double checked I had the Euros that Hertogen had given me. I stepped into the end of the taxi rank line and after half an hour was safely at my hotel.

It was a cool, dry day and I was impressed as we had passed through the city, through the European quarter and into the heart of the EU. Art Deco sat next to medieval, a city very much in the present, with one foot in the past. We passed the university, where I had heard that the day before, some students had pulled down a statue of Leopold. The right wing might have been on the rise, but imperialism apparently was not. My hotel, the Hotel de to Malstracken, to give it its opulent name, also boasted a very opulent interior. I'd say it was easily the finest I had been in, if you like that type of thing. I could smoke in my room, which was one of the best parts for me.

"Pardon, Excusé, Ou Est Le Royal Museum a la fine arts?" I asked in my 'pigeon with a stutter' French.

"Speak English," came the gruff reply.

He must have been Flemish I figured. Still proud of my B in GCSE French, it couldn't have been the fault of my language skills. He pointed the way anyhow and I crossed a large park and over towards the museum. I suppose it'd be like a foreigner going to the Shankill and speaking Gaelic at some fella in a Rangers top. Hertogen had said to go sightseeing on the first day and that he wouldn't have anything for me to do until at least the second. I thought I'd do as I was told.

I spent an hour or two, idling around, doing the tourist thing. I was enjoying myself. Some of the art I found a wee bit boring, but it was preferable to the batshit crazy Magritte stuff that was being advertised all over the place—I wouldn't be visiting there. They looked like later day Pink Floyd covers to me. I sat down on a leather sofa in the centre of one of the galleries and almost lit up a smoke. A no smoking sign caught my eye. I suppose they had to ban it somewhere. I was due a pill and took it out and popped it. I looked around at the huge portraits in the room, housed in massive gilt and golden frames, everything at least a hundred years old. No Percy French's there. In saying that, I liked his stuff just as much. I'm not claiming to be any expert. They say this is the era of experts, though I'm not even an expert on Brian Caskey.

As I sat there, a few couples came past, families too. A young pair with a little boy ambled past and they all smiled at me. I smiled back. It was funny. I got a little pang in my stomach. Suddenly I thought about how alone I was. Jeez, I said to myself, where did that come from? It hit me like a ton of shite. Had I gone to places like this with Mary and Sean? I didn't know. Would those memories return one day? I shivered. That was something I didn't want, I don't want. I pushed it all from my mind. I was essentially being paid to be on holiday, I'd enjoy it, things would keep getting better, end of story. I shook myself and the nausea passed. I got up and crossed to a smaller portrait of a man in an oval mount, mid yawn. I yawned back. Why does that always happen? I bet you're yawning reading this.

Chapter Thirty-Eight

"*T*he police should be here presently," said Parsons, *gathering himself. He pulled off his spectacles and began to clean them on his jacket tails.*

"*Suicide?*" the maitre d' whispered to me, wide eyed.

"*It looks that way,*" I replied.

I got down on my honkers beside the body and pulled out a pen. I carefully pulled back Gallagher's saturated blue jacket a little to get a better look at the wound. It was so large that it was impossible to tell where each shot had hit him, if both had actually struck him. All I was going on was the noise. I felt his neck to be sure he was dead, there was no pulse, but he was still warm. I stood up and walked over to the wall behind, feeling my hands over the wall. There was no sign of any exit damage, the bullets could still have been in him, I figured. I crouched back down beside the body and placed two fingers on the semi-automatic barrel of the gun.

"*Don't touch it!*" rasped Parsons, regaining his authority.

I stood again, unfazed. "Look, I don't think I'm a suspect here, unless I managed to shoot around corners and a couple of doors while eating my dinner. I wanted to see if it's still warm. It isn't."

"*What for?*" broke in the maitre d', still high on his nerves.

"It's just a bit strange. No smell of burnt powder either."

"*Surely you don't think that he was murdered?*" said Parsons incredulously.

"*I don't know to be honest,*" I said stiffly.

"Is it not bad enough that one of our staff is a thief and has killed himself on site?" he said, blinking profusely.

"Bad enough?" I asked evenly. *"Pretty bad for Gallagher."*

He held out his glasses, wiped them, and tutted. *"You know what I mean, this is a terrible business."*

I walked across to the windows and inspected them thoroughly, running my hands over the glass.

"Surely a bullet would have shattered the glass," continued Parsons. *"The room was locked from both sides too, I think it clear what happened here."*

I ignored him until I was sure there was nothing suspicious about the glass. I moved up the room, searching as I went. By the time I got to the back door again, the banging had stopped. Hopefully someone had told them what had happened. I headed back towards my two companions.

"So, what exactly is clear?" I asked.

"Well, I suppose... I suppose, Gallagher must have returned to the scene of his crime and then, well, shot himself," Parsons responded irritably.

"Why?"

"Well, I don't know. You're the detective. I'm not a thief, I don't know what was going through his mind."

I sighed. *"I'm gonna get a bit of fresh air and a cigarette, anyone care to join me?"*

"Yes, I'd like to get out of here," said the maitre d'.

"I am going to await the police," Parsons said with a sniff.

"That's fine, best not touch anything," I said, walking on by and ignoring his flushed, irate expression.

***

"I think you know I'm Billy, what's your name again?" I said, lighting up a number.

"John Cole," the maitre d' informed me.

We were smoking out by the back gardens, just beyond the terrace. I think we both wanted to put some distance from the hotel for a minute.

"What do you think about it all?" I asked.

"I'm not sure. It seems like he, sadly, took his own life. But, you're right to look into it and, of course, I'm sure the police will." He spoke rapidly, taking in drags, in between syllables.

"Yeah," I said absently.

After a few minutes, we watched two police cars winding up the driveway, no sirens, just headlights.

***

We walked back inside the hotel silently. Inside, there was a thin murmur and everyone talked in hushed whispers, with concerned expressions. The staff tried to put on brave faces and guests didn't much bother. We walked back to the Leopold room where the door was shut and two officers were standing in front of it.

"Hello John," said the first, as we stopped outside.

"Hello Frank, a terrible thing," he said.

"It is, it is. This here is Billy Chapman, a private detective. He was with us when we found the body."

Both officers gave me a firm nod and regarded me like a scuff on their shoe.

"Okay if we go back inside?" asked John.

"That's fine," said the first man opening the door for us. "Inspector Stark is in there with Mr. Parsons."

We entered and the door closed behind us. More lights had been turned on and the room's atmosphere became a mix of harsh light and shadows. Parsons and Stark were in conversation, standing over the body, with their backs to us. After a few seconds, they both turned around.

"This is John, our maitre d', and Mr. Chapman, a... um, private detective," Parsons said, tailing off.

The new man was in his late forties, wearing a dark green suit, a black trench coat, and with a lit pipe in one hand. He had thinning black hair and was cleanly shaven. His voice had a thick country edge, with a sharp underside.

"Hello, I'm Inspector Stark," he said to me. "Hello John," he added, turning.

"Hello, good to see you, pity about the circumstances," replied John.

"Good to know you," I said, and held out my hand.

He shook it. "Private detective huh, never been with our outfit?" he asked.

"No," I said, "I started this up after leaving the army."

"Oh?" he said and puffed on his pipe. "Which regiment?"

"Irish Guards, Second Division."

He nodded and let out a thin smile. "Were you in France?"

"I was," I said.

"Me too," he said with a knowing smile.

That was enough, we didn't need any more background talk. We had the cut of one another.

"What do you think about poor Gallagher?" he asked, gesturing with his pipe.

I was a little off balance for an instant, I wasn't much used to police wanting to hear my opinions.

"It appears pretty cut and dry, but I'm not sure. Obviously it could well be a suicide. I think we can rule out an accident."

"Go on," he said receptively.

"A few things point to the theory of it being a murder," I said and Parsons snorted. "For a start, I don't get why he would slip back in here to murder himself. I don't know many suicides where a guy shoots himself in the chest and then does it again right after, either. I don't like

how far away that gun was on the floor from the body. It was ice cold too."

He smiled almost benevolently, and said, "But the doors were both locked shut. Anyone running out after a murder would most likely have been seen too. There's no cracks in the windows and the openings are too high and small for someone to have climbed in or shot through..."

"I didn't say it was a great theory."

"Fair enough," he said.

Chapter Thirty-Nine

I had my laptop out with me and I chose a nice little café, away from the busiest parts of the museum district. The young girl behind the counter smiled pleasantly and perhaps indulgently as I asked for 'Une café' and 'One of those, sil vous plait,' pointing at something very chocolatey and biscuity. Setting myself up by the window, I did a bit of editing first, nothing too taxing.

Look at me, I thought, *a writer sitting in a café on the continent. Hemmingway himself.* Well, he allegedly had said "write drunk, edit sober." My mantra was most often, "write drunk, edit drunk." I'd go easy on the drink, I'd been cutting back okay. The cigs weren't going so well, especially cause I was struggling to take up vaping. Oh well. I enjoyed the moment anyhow. Things could have been worse, a lot worse. After a pretty severe breakdown, here I was, less than a year later, on an interesting case, expenses paid, writing another novel. *Look at me, Ma*!

***

I spent the late part of the afternoon just walking about, taking the air and cigarette smoke, and enjoying the smells of a new city. The air smelt a little bit different, it felt colder too, and there was a pleasant mix of freshly cooked food from the many stalls. I came across a small church— Gothic architecture I'd say, though I'm no expert—with a sign in English that said, 'Please come in.' I had nothing better to do. I did as I was told, like Alice being told, 'Drink me.'

It was empty inside, and cold, dark and echoey. I sat down at the edge of a pew and took a moment. The silence was beautiful. The interior was beautiful too, overpowering and heavy, and well, unnecessary, but kind of cool. It wasn't much like the church I was dragged to as a kid, every Sunday. It had been a gospel hall, outside the estate. There wasn't time for much peace or reflection there. It was all shouty, "You're gonna burn," "you need to be saved," real 'end is nigh' stuff. I shivered, not from the cold, and left.

I ended up in Grand Place as it started to get dark. It is a well preserved medieval square, enclosed by tall, ornate buildings, surviving wars, invasions, and revolutions. I wondered if it would survive the next fifty years. I thought I would try walking back to my hotel and got completely lost. I mistook the city centre as being something on the scale of say Prague, but found it was much, much bigger. I chanced upon the Comic Museum, with huge posters of Tin Tin lining the windows. They were just closing up and I made a mental note to try and pay a visit before I left. I was tired. I figured my expenses bill could take another hit and found a taxi rank.

I was back at my hotel for about seven and crawled up to my room, wrecked, but with a nice kind of tiredness. I treated myself to room service, a local delicacy of cheeseburger and chips. I'm certain they had it on the menu just for the Yanks and Brits. My room was super fancy, but the luxury was liveable, you could relax in it. No teas-maid mind. I ordered up a litre of some local frothy goodness and it tasted amazing. I put on CNN and lay down on the bed, with one of the bedside lights faintly illuminating the large space. I fell into a deep sleep.

***

I jolted up when my phone rang, my heart jumping out of my chest and racing along the floor. I slugged the residue of my beer and sat up straight. Hertogen. And the screen also said 9.36 p.m.

"Hello?"

"Mr. Caskey, I hope you are well."

"Yes, yes, good thank you. And yourself?"

"Very good. Now, how are you enjoying my country?"

"Great," I said and stifled a cough, the countless smokes of the day repeating on me. "It's a lovely city."

"Good. It most certainly is. Now, your meeting will be tomorrow with the gentleman I told you about," he said, his tone a pitch higher.

That would be a guy I would only know as Jahn. He was the one they had on the inside.

"He will meet you at one p.m. at the agreed location."

Hertogen had informed me previously that a flyer for a well-known tourist spot would be posted under my door during the night, informing me where to go.

"I trust that is agreeable Mr. Caskey?"

"Yeah, of course, grand. I'll look forward to it. Good night."

"Have a restful sleep," he said softly.

I rubbed my eyes and decided I didn't want to sit up stressing all night. I plugged in my laptop and drafted up a couple of chapters. I turned in before midnight and fell into a deep, hard, dreamless sleep.

***

When I woke up, the first thing I did was to grab the hotel phone, and ring down for a pot of coffee. I pulled back the covers, hot from the dry heat that was pumping out of the radiators. Sure enough, there was a flyer on the floor by the door. I picked it up, groaning as I leaned over—it was for Mini-Europe. I had heard of the place—cool, I thought. Maybe my meds were squiffy, but I was enjoying playing like I was James Bond. I sure smoked enough and drank enough to be Fleming's Bond, but I admit I lacked his acumen. Okay, so I was going to meet some undercover guy and then follow some other guy who was called Blakey, though neither of them would be their real names, fine. I showered, shaved and dressed, and went down for my continental breakfast.

***

I walked on past Maalbeek Station, wanting to have a look at the centre of the EU. My sausages and fruit salad nestled nicely in my stomach and the coffee had woken me up at least a crack. I had had them separately, I'm not that crazy. There were flowers outside the station, some new, some wilting. It had been the scene of the devastating terrorist bomb a few years previously and probably had been lined with foliage ever since. I stopped and sat down, had a little ponder and a little smoke, before walking on. As I neared the EU hub, there was an influx of busy looking men and women in suits, being busy, looking busy. I stood up and had another smoke, surveying the large Char building. It's an impressive thing certainly. Funny to think though, that it's been where all of these ancient nations have had to bend the knee. Well, that's what the Brexiteers would say anyway. I looked at my cigarette with part disgust, stubbing it out and stamping it into oblivion. I knew I needed to cut down.

I walked on and by late morning, I was at Bruparck and approaching Mini-Europe. I paid my admission, noting the price for later, and headed in. I was faintly staggered by the Atomium on the hill, in the background. I stopped still and shoved my hands into my jean pockets. It's a crazy, incongruous looking structure, like something Gerry Anderson might have made after a toke. It's basically a construction of tubes and balls that intersect high up in the air, a restaurant is even inside one of them. It was apparently built in the fifties, though it looks like it would have been ahead of its time for The Jetsons.

I began my walk around the park and pulled my collar close to me as a skiff of snow came on. I passed Big Ben, next to the Eiffel Tower, then the Coliseum. I never did do any backpacking before. I stopped at Vesuvius, as it actually began to erupt.

"Mr. Caskey, please walk with me."

"Oh, sure," I said, flustered, and then getting into mode and forgetting the fate of Pompei.

We walked past Amsterdam and Venice before either of us spoke again. Jahn was medium height, a brown tinge in skin tone, with short hair and a thick beard. The beard made it harder to tell, but I'd say he was in his early thirties. We stopped next to a knight suit mock up that tourists could stand behind and have their pictures taken at.

"So, you know we want you to follow this guy a little bit?" he said in a French or maybe Belgian accent. The snow had stopped and he dusted flakes off his jeans in a light motion and opened the zip on his black leather jacket. His eyes darted about as he waited for me to respond.

"Yeah, Hertogen said."

"No names please," he said evenly and glanced around again.

"Ok, sorry," I said and shrugged, pulling out a smoke. "When and where?"

"We have intelligence that he is going to be in Bruges tomorrow, getting in by train at three thirty-five in the afternoon."

I nodded, smoking, and my attention turned to a mother and her young son, looking to squeeze past us and pose for some photos. Jahn and I exchanged looks and we walked on towards London again. Maybe we could take in a show.

"That's fine, so you want me to follow him and then what? Hand over to someone or stay with him while he's there, how does it work?"

"We want you to stay with him for as long as possible. We do not have the manpower to survey him at all times. You may well lose him at some point, or if he seems to be staying for the night, you are free to leave and travel back to your hotel."

"Just leave?" I said, with some confusion. "Then what?"

"Then, we will contact you again the following day," he said and took out a piece of nicotine gum and began to chew it. Maybe he had given up the smokes when he had gone under cover.

"Okay, I get it, if that's all you want for now, no problem," I said. It seemed off though; maybe they really didn't have much government support and manpower. Seemed a strange thing to bring me all the way over for, but maybe there'd be something else later. Or maybe I was being tested?

"Keep your eyes peeled, especially if there is anyone you recognise or might have seen during your surveillance in Belfast."

"Yes, will do."

"Here's a recent picture of... you know," he said and passed it over. "Looks a bit different from the passport photo you saw, keep it on you to be certain."

"Okay, thanks, I will."

"Okay good," he said and licked his lips. "Any questions?"

"Yeah," I said, and pointed up at the Atomium, looming on the hill. "Seriously, what the fuck is that about?"

Chapter Forty

I *hadn't been in a peeler car for years. Stark had been more than up for cooperation, a welcome attitude for a man who surely knew he was skilled. Perhaps he also knew that two heads were better than one, even if it was a private head.*

"Just up this road," said Parsons to the officer driving.

Stark had agreed for myself and Parsons to accompany him, along with another officer, to a first search of Gallagher's home. It was cold in the car and the windows had begun to steam up, as the first drops of rain bounced off their outside. It was only ten minutes in the car and the last few were spent in silence. Stark was in the front seat. His back looked thoughtful, maybe the creases in his coat looked like a face. I could see the puff-puff of his pipe smoke, crawling up the window, to meet the mist of condensation.

"I could book you for withholding information you know," he said casually as we walked up to the small house. It sat at the end of a nice enough terrace, on the edge of the countryside.

"Yeah, I know," I said simply.

"Parsons filled me in on your arrangement with McBride and Fotheringay," he continued. "I could book the lot of you."

"If it helps, I'd have called you guys after the first gunshot."

"Thanks," he said, with a mild guffaw.

The other two approached as we all gathered around the front door, the officer carrying some kind of metal ram.

"Gwan ahead Trevor," said Stark.

Trevor lunged at the door with it twice, and on the third go, the wood splintered away from the lock. He gave it a final kick open, which I'm sure was quite satisfying. Stark led the way, turned on the lights, and went into the small sitting room. He indicated for Trevor to start a search upstairs. I followed Stark inside, as Parsons stood awkwardly in the hall, fidgeting with his lapels. There wasn't much to find, he had lived simply enough and it was tidy. In the kitchen, dishes were awaiting putting away and an ashtray needed emptying. The walls were a sickly lime green and the kitchen could have done with a major makeover.

"Sir, you'll want to see this," came a muffled shout from upstairs. Parsons followed Stark and myself up the stairs, the three wise men of Newcastle. There was no baby Jesus up the stairs. What there was, were nine framed paintings sitting on top of the spare bed, in the small second room. Stark just puffed solemnly on his pipe, but Parsons let out a self-satisfied, "Ha!"

I walked over to the pictures and lifted a few off. I moved the first two or three to the side on the faded white linen, now more like cream. There it was, 'The Hound of Ulster.' It was a kill for the poet.

Chapter Forty-One

'In Bruges.' That's where I was. I love that film. If I had any friends I might have texted them that. The first café I visited, I had a coffee and cake, with a trio of chocolate that was awesome. The second café was superb too, and it continued like that until café number three almost finished me, and it was only lunch time. I had gotten there early and ambled around the cobbled roads between coffees. It's a bloody incredible place. It's actually preserved as a medieval town, hard to believe really. I had hours left to kill and thought I'd make the most of it. I walked over the canal bridge, past the old town hall, when a heavy snow started, just as I arrived at the Bosch exhibition. I spent an hour or so there and half wished I was still sixteen and had a bag of magic mushies. It's some mad shit! I quite liked it, but it's crazy none the less, stilts coming out of eyes and little devils running around in the snow, I don't know what he was on. Anyway, I thought I'd better get myself together and had yet another coffee and went for a leak. It cost me three Euros just for the piss.

Enough merrymaking I decided, time to get into gear. I felt a bit jittery, in part it was probably all the caffeine, though I took an extra one of my pills just in case. I was sitting in the station an hour early, ready with an English newspaper, a packet of smokes, and good intentions. Blakey was one of the first to come out from the gates, a few minutes after the arrival time. I pulled out the photo to check and was satisfied, shoving it back into my pocket. I was wearing a black duffel coat and I began to do up the buttons, ready to head back into the cold. My quarry passed near to my bench, his hair had grown slightly longer and a navy baseball cap all but covered it. He also had on blue jeans and a green jacket, with a white fluffy hood.

As I stepped outside, I was greeted by the hustle and smells of the town and my heart raced a little, probably from the thrill of the chase. I stopped near the door and made a fuss of lighting up a cig as I saw him stop and look around, and then walk on quickly in the direction of the oldest part of town. I took a drag and then with a skip, strode on, anxious not to be seen, but also not to lose him. I knew that they had said it was okay if I lost him after a time, though I still couldn't quite get my head around that.

He went on alone, past the modern shops and then the little chocolatiers, closer to the medieval section. We passed churches, bridges over canals, and at least five or six buildings I could recall from In Bruges. There was no time for location spotting. His first stop was at a café. It was on a fairly busy side street and I crossed the road to see what he would do next. He reappeared and sat down at an outside table, with a cup of coffee and a slice of something. I ducked into one of the cafés opposite and took an inside window seat, where I could just about keep tabs on him. I ordered a coke this time and nothing to eat. I don't know why, it probably had more caffeine anyway, but I was trying to keep myself on an even keel.

Before a quarter of an hour had passed, he was up and walking again. I nonchalantly followed, keeping a good few metres behind, pretending to take an interest in shop fronts and some of the old buildings. He walked on purposefully, occasionally glancing to his side or behind him. This went on for about ten minutes and then, BANG! I was about to step out to cross a side street, a bit behind Blakey, when a white van sped up and then pulled up abruptly, just beside me. He blocked my path and view, the swarm of tourists, squeezing past either side of the van, blocking me in further. I shot a look inside and could just make out a bit of face behind the dirty glass; a beanie hat and sunglasses were covering most of his face. He glanced at me, looked away and then slowly moved off again. I scrambled around the back of him, trying to use the van as leverage to push past the hustle of people moving in both directions, crossing between the two roads. My eyes shot in every direction. The noise of outside swam deafeningly through my ears. Blakey was nowhere to be seen. Fuck.

Once I was safely on the other side of the road, I stopped dead again and searched all around—no sign. A few people pushed past me, as I stood motionless in their way. I went on down the road in the direction that Blakey had seemed to be going, at a canter. My brow felt sticky. I felt clammy under my jacket. The streets were busy, most looked like tourists. I stopped again, breathing hard. Shite—nothing. When I got to another bridge, I stopped and looked across from where I had a fairly good view of the street ahead. No Blakey.

I ran back to where I had first lost him, the last few cigarettes starting to rattle around some in my chest. The street off to the right had a few tat shops, selling postcards and chocolate, and I ran up there. A few faces eyed my own now sweaty face suspiciously, as I ran past them. I got to another crossroads and I was beginning to stray outside the touristy area. The unwanted feeling began to grow inside me, that that was it, I had lost him. I ran my hands through my hair a couple of times. The houses were newer and more residential looking. Bollox, he could have been anywhere. I chose a street and made one last run. It lasted about thirty seconds and I wheezed past a few pedestrians, and then stopped half way along. I decided I'd bite the bullet early on and get it over with. I took out my phone and rang the last number that Hertogen had contacted me on.

"The number you have dialled has not been recognised," the voice informed me. I wished I'd had a proper number I could call, but all this cloak and dagger shit meant I had none. Fuck this! I gave my shoulders a half-hearted shrug, and lit up a smoke. I coughed hard and bent over a little. I straightened up and took a good pull on the smoke and things felt better. I felt sweaty in my jacket, but noticed the cold on my neck for the first time since my fun run. I was roasting, but out in the snow.

I walked back on myself to the previous crossroads and sauntered along a new road, I decided that I may as well. I was annoyed at myself, though more annoyed at that stupid van driver. I supposed it wasn't the end of the world, I'd still get paid they had said. I wanted to find something though, I wanted to Jason Bourne it across Europe.

I was almost finished my smoke and was starting to think about where I'd go for dinner when—*Fuck me! Is that him?* Down the end of a quiet road, just down from where I was, walked a figure, the same clothes, the same build, about fifty metres away. I sped up and stared towards him, my eyes were surely boring right into his back. I tried to still blend in, in the quiet street best I could. *It is him*, I decided. "Fucking right," I whispered.

My heart stepped up a few beats too. When he was about thirty metres away from me, he took out a key and let himself into a terrace building, a few doors up from the park. I couldn't believe my luck. I crossed the road and made as if I was aiming for the park gates. I neared the entrance and decided that I was best to go on through. As I did, I clocked a van down a side street, off to my right. A white van, the same markings as the one from earlier.

Chapter Forty-Two

"Thanks for stopping for a drink," said Stark, as we both sipped a ten-year-old malt, in the snug of the Slieve Donard.

"No problem," I said, "I don't need much convincing. And another thing," I paused and fixed him in the eye, "I appreciate your cutting me into things."

"It makes sense," he replied plainly and took another swig of his whiskey. "What's your take on the paintings?"

"Very neat and tidy," I said.

"Yes it is."

We both drank a bit more and I fingered out a cigarette, while he prepared another toke.

"You know, McBride has quite a bit of influence locally," he said softly.

"Yeah, so I heard."

"I'm suspicious of things like you, but I don't see anything to hang on anyone right about now. First thing tomorrow, my tiny little country force is going to have a lot of pressure to wrap this up. And they'll want it tidy."

"I know they will."

"I might need someone else to dig a little bit more on things. Someone outside."

"I think you will."

***

At breakfast the next morning, there was an atmosphere of something between a wake and Christmas Eve. Staff were trying to appear chipper enough as they hurried about, but it didn't look right. Nothing looked right. Something had changed. Even the dining room suddenly looked dated and in need of freshening up too, and the coffee didn't taste strong enough. Maybe that was just me. I must say though the fry still tasted all right. It'd take a lot more to put me off my breakfast.

"Good morning, Mr. Chapman," came a voice in my ear. I had been watching the rain drizzling against the window pane beside my table, it hadn't stopped all night. It was McBride.

"Mr. McBride, my condolences," I said standing and offering my hand. We shook.

"Thank you, please, may I sit?" he asked, frowning.

"Of course, please," I said and indicated the chair opposite.

"Terrible, just terrible," he said, looking around the restaurant and then settling his eyes onto mine.

"It certainly is," I said, meeting his gaze.

His wide frame somewhat monopolised the table, as he leaned over and then spoke quieter.

"I also hope that you are not upset in being, well, embroiled in this business."

"Think nothing of it," I said, shrugging.

"Yes, but I hear that Mr. Stark is somewhat annoyed at our discretion," he looked away, "perhaps our indiscretion. Of course, we couldn't possibly have known how things would end up."

"Of course," I said, not sure where he was going with all of this.

"I will straighten things out and of course take full responsibility."

He puffed out his cheeks and issued me a firm nod.

"That shouldn't be necessary, but thank you," I offered, reaching out my first smoke of the day. He smiled at me and then it was his turn to peer out at the morning drizzle.

"You arrived much earlier than I expected," I said, flicking the flint of my lighter.

"Yes, I of course spoke with Fotheringay last night and I took the very first train out this morning. He dropped me to the hotel, kindly, just a few minutes ago."

He patted his legs and leaned forwards.

"I do not want to disturb your breakfast any further. We can have a chat for elevens if that suits you?"

"Of course."

"I must speak with Mr. Parsons and then Mr. Stark. I will meet you in the residents' lounge then."

"That's fine," I said, as he heavily moved himself up out of the chair and out towards the lobby. I stubbed out the cigarette, it was much too early.

***

The meeting took place close to time, Stark, Fotheringay, and Parsons were there too. Stark gave us a light grilling, but I expect it was more for show than anything. He informed us that the likely outcome would be that of suicide, but that it would take a week or two of standard investigation. He then left with Parsons to look over some documents. He nodded his hat to me as he left.

That left the three of us, and Fotheringay closed the door behind them.

"Sadly, it seems that the verdict is quite clear," said Fotheringay, lighting up one of his Wintermans.

"Yes, it does," I said.

"If he had been in such dire distress, I wish that he would have come to me," spoke McBride, with a somewhat pained expression. "So very sad."

"We have spoken with Inspector Stark, prior to just now I mean," broke in Fotheringay. "You should not receive any official reproach."

"Yes, yes that's just fine," I said. "Look, do you want me to investigate anything further?"

They looked at one another. "I think there is no need, the paintings were found in his home and he was the only real suspect. Unfortunately, the case has been concluded."

"Yes," cut in McBride. "We thank you for your time and again our apologies for this involvement. We have your wages and a little extra besides," he said, setting a brown envelope down on the table. "Please feel free to stay another night or two, for your trouble."

"As our guest," added Fotheringay.

"Thanks, I think I will stay a little longer. Thank you both and good luck."

I thought I detected a flicker on Fotheringay's face.

***

*T*he next few days were strange. The hotel returned to a faded photostat of normality. I didn't get to have much face time with Stark, and the case had been taken somewhat out of his hands. I didn't see much of my former employers either and when I did, I felt like an ex-lover that was now regarded with some shame. Parsons did not seem enamoured by my presence either, not so much an invited guest, as an unwanted one.

I was left to my thoughts and I had several. Had Gallagher just killed himself? The locked doors, the gun beside him, the dramatic set up. It just didn't feel right. But what was the alternative? Did McBride or Fotheringay want him dead—why would they? Stark had told me that what little estate Gallagher had, it was only a cousin that would benefit. And what would Fotheringay care? How about Parsons—was there a reason to do with the hotel, that he could resort to murder? I didn't really think so. The maitre d'? No, I had lots of thoughts, but no conclusions.

"Will you have a whiskey with me?" said Stark on my final night.

"I've told you, you can take it as read," I said with a wink.

We had a few, and a few more besides.

"It looks set for Tuesday that the verdict will be given. Straight suicide. I pressed for an open verdict, but no dice."

"I thought that's the way it would go."

"It was going to be really. But you're still suspicious?"

"Yeah, are you not?"

"I am, I don't know what's gone on there, to be honest. There's nobody I could imagine getting the pinch on for it. I can't even prove it was murder."

"What about the bullet wounds? Surely it wouldn't have made that kind of mess at close range."

"I didn't think it looked right either, but there's nothing conclusive about it."

"Did the gun check out that it was the one that fired? It was cold."

"It matches the bullets, and it had been fired. There's no telling when though."

"A bit weird, seeing an American Browning out here in the sticks."

"We couldn't read the register on it, the digits were too worn. Or maybe they had been sanded down some. Gallagher wasn't registered as having a permit, but then he wouldn't be the first either."

"And the toxicology?"

"He was steaming drunk it appears, or he had a huge immunity to the drink. Nothing else showed up though."

"How about the paintings?"

"His prints were on them, nobody else's."

"Is that not a little strange too?"

"It is, but again, nothing conclusive."

"And the will?"

"It goes to his cousin who seems pretty upset, but by the time the funeral is paid for and a few debts, it'll only be a small sum."

We chewed over it all for a moment.

He gave his head a short shake.

"If back in Belfast, you choose to do a little more snooping, no one is going to stop you," he said quietly, looking down at his tobacco tin, pulling out a new thread for his cooling pipe.

"I think I might."

"Good," he said casually, pushing across a white envelope between our two shorts.

"Towards your expenses and for your help this week," he said.

Chapter Forty-Three

I walked on through the gates of the park. Nobody had been in the van, of that I was fairly sure. So, if I was right, whoever was in that van was probably already inside the house. *What the fuck is going on*, I asked myself. Something was really off beam. Or, maybe I was wrong, and it had been a different van. But I was pretty sure, my Norn Iron *Spidey* sense was tingling. So someone knew who I was? Or at least what I was up to? Maybe not, but with the van blocking me like that, it did make sense.

Nausea swept gurgling through my stomach, but I forced it away. What trouble had I get myself involved in? And, in a foreign country? I reminded myself that I hadn't broken any laws yet, here or back home. Not yet anyway. I was able to amble around the gates for a while without drawing attention to myself. I was out of sight from the house, but could view the path up to the front door. I couldn't just walk away and leave it. I smoked a few cigarettes and waited.

About twenty minutes later, I crept along the inside path a bit, to see if I could get a look at the back of the house. I counted three in and could just see a little of the upstairs window, above a six-foot-high fence. Each house had a gate leading onto the park. There was a tree-lined path beside and I went over, pretending to be trying to get a signal on my phone. I registered the lock and could see the metal of a padlock on the oval cut out. I moved closer, seeing as no one was around, and found the trees were almost bare against it. I could see through to a small garden at the rear of the house. There was a window with blinds open on one room. There was another small window built into the back door. I stood still and thought hard, deciding.

I could squeeze through between the trees if I wanted to. It was getting quite dark, I could give it a go. Why not Jason Bond?

For some reason that's exactly what I did do. I wish now that I hadn't. I inched past each tree, trying to avoid any noise, and made it to the edge of the garden. I kept low and crossed, hiding momentarily behind some more trees. There was no sign of anyone around. I ran that last part and ducked down at the back wall, just to the side of the large window. My chest was heaving and I forced some vomit back down. I inched left until I was below the window. I peeped up like a particularly meek Meer cat to chance a look, but the blinds were closed tight.

Then I heard shouting. I shot down again, tense and frightened. What was I doing? Had they heard me? Then I realised the shouts were at each other and the only interest was in one another. I couldn't make anything out and the language didn't seem to be English. I half crawled along the gravel ground and over to the back door. I paused and wiped the dirt and stones off my palms. I could hear the voices more clearly, echoey. I figured there were two rooms there, it was maybe an attached kitchen. I peered in through the bottom right corner and sure enough it was a kitchen and it was empty. The voices were coming through the connecting open door. I looked across; my stomach heaved at what I saw. Inside, there was Jahn, tied to a chair, face cut and bleeding. Standing over him was Blakey, a knife in his hand.

***

I watched for a minute or so as Blakey first set the knife down, shouted some kind of questions at Jahn, waited in silence, and then rained down a series of blows onto Jahn's face. I could hear Jahn's groans, muffled through the glass. He then shook his head and repeated some small sentence I didn't understand, over and over. He was partially slumped and looked to be struggling to stay conscious. Blakey picked up the knife and began to shout again, waving it around wildly.

My hand moved to the back-door handle on instinct, and to my surprise, it opened. I crept in, Blakey with his back to me and his raised voice hiding any sound that I was making. I padded out of sight, into the small kitchen, and searched for any possible weapon. There was a long, thin bread knife by the sink, and I grabbed that. I moved back towards the door and looked in, making eye contact with Jahn.

Blakey seemed to sense something and spun around. I lunged into the room. I kicked Blakey hard in the back as he was turning, hoping to knock the knife from his hand. He fell down on one knee and shot up again, still clutching his knife. I stumbled, slightly off balance, and then caught sight of Jahn's face, eyes pleading, veins bulging. Blakey swiped up at me in one movement and sliced the underside of my left arm. It instantly started to bleed, but it was only a nick.

I caught my balance and returned a swipe, cutting down on the wrist that was holding the knife. It had dug into his skin and he dropped the knife, some blood running down after it. There was a long pause, neither of us sure of the next move. The next second he was on me. He had sprung up and pushed my arms back, pinning me against the wall behind. He punched me hard in the face and I dropped my own knife. Instinct from my teens kicked in and I head butted him, cracking him on the bridge of his nose. He stepped backwards, blood pissing from his nostrils. I punched him hard in the stomach and pushed on past him, looking for more space. He composed himself yet again and clawed at me from the side, his eyes wild in his head. He got in a few blows, including a hard hook to my cheek. I went down on the floor, him behind me, beating any part of me that he could get at. He half mounted me, punching and scrabbing, as I tried to crawl further towards Jahn and away from the beating.

Then there was his knife, a few inches from my hand. I cut out all the pain going to my brain and only focused on clawing closer to the knife. I could feel my own blood, warm and sticky, open wounds now on my back. It was almost touching my fingers. In the last instant, I plucked it up, twisted half on my back and plunged the blade into his chest, right up to the hilt. The noise he made was almost a shriek and his sweating face was aghast as it looked down at the blade below his ribs. He fell backwards, blood only tricking out, but the damage was done. I fell onto my knees and breathed hard and laboured. After a few seconds, he was dead.

Chapter Forty-Four

I *had only been back in Belfast a night, when the grim surroundings were depressing me beyond reason. Or maybe it was just the business in Newcastle. I took myself off to Bangor for the day and to the Tonic Cinema. The seaside town had changed a bit since the Vikings had invaded and when its abbey was one of the most famous in the world. It hadn't changed all that much though since the Victorians. It still had its piers and beaches and donkey rides. One newer thing it did have was the largest picture house in all of Ireland. It held two and half thousand people and even sold chewing gum, which had recently been introduced to us by all the Yanks who had been stationed here.*

I had previously enjoyed 'Laura' and was glad to see another Otto Preminger film was showing, 'Whirlpool.' I actually managed to switch off for a few hours and immersed myself in the big screen, and a story involving hypnosis and psychosis. It was a good suspense movie too.

I ate a chicken and ham pie in the café afterwards, which was attached to the large, white Deco building. It was a good day. Solitary, but that's often the way I like it. The last train was to leave at ten and allowed me a quick stop off on High Street for a pint of stout and a few cigs. Once on the train, as East Belfast got closer, I felt tense and uneasy. I'd do a bit of digging the next day, I decided. It was a bad end to the day. Though I was tired, I turned and turned in bed, pulling off sheets, heaving them on again, unable to sleep.

***

The next morning was a Wednesday and I stopped off at the market at Saint George's. It was a hive and had been building itself back into a diverse hub during those post war years. I busied myself the rest of the day, stopping off at Great Victoria Street Station, the Public Records Office, the War and Military Office, the Works and Pensions Bureau, the Central Hotel, and the Crown Bar. All were for business purposes. I called in on my Glentoran contact as well, John Neil, to see if I could find anything of interest about McBride. He was either just being cagey, or he had nothing to tell. He certainly didn't seem to welcome my questions.

I crawled back into my dank and really fairly grotty office in Sydenham at around six. I sat back with a cigarette and surveyed the many pages I had filled in my notepad. I was casting a wide net and was trying to find any leads to do with any of the main players. Here are some of the notes I took:

Gallagher—Seemed to have lived in Newcastle most of his life, some time spent in England, no war record, no sign of illegitimate children, no criminal record.

Parsons—Worked at hotel most of life, Home Guard war record—nothing of interest, wife, two children, some business shares.

Cole—Worked at hotel about ten years, no war record, one caution from 1935 for drunk and disorderly, married, no children.

Fotheringay—Various business shares, worked for McBride for 5 years, not married or children, no criminal record, served in army 1929-1934, ending career as Corporal.

McBride—Business owner much of life, various board and shareholder positions, army record 1922-1930—ending career as a Colour Sergeant, no criminal record. No record of pre-booking train journey on day of arrival in Newcastle.

There were a few interesting tit bits, but nothing to take to Stark as yet.

***

Two days later the postman brought me a parcel. He usually only gave me brown envelopes with things like 'Final Warning' written on them. It was a rectangle about two feet by one, padded inside and wrapped in brown string. I didn't get many Christmas or birthday presents, and took my time over this. I couldn't think what it would be. I peeled off layers of thick brown paper and discovered the back of a brown mahogany frame. I turned it over to find a watercolour was housed inside. It was an unfinished smaller version of 'The Hound of Ulster.' It looked wonderful, the rawness not detracting from its beauty. There was a note accompanying it.

"Dear Mr. Chapman, I hope you will accept a small token of our gratitude and appreciation. Thanks to you again in assisting in resolving the case to a close. I remembered your admiration of Percy French and although not of substantial value, I hope it will be of pleasure to you.

Faithfully,

McBride"

He hadn't necessarily been at the top of my list for further investigation, but he was now.

Chapter Forty-Five

My breathing settled and I shook myself. My body hurt like all hell. Jahn and I were yet to speak. It was like an awkward silence with a stranger, following some kind of deviant sexual encounter. I pulled myself up and stood over the body. I shook my head and then looked over towards Jahn, his face a bloody pulp, but nothing life threatening.

"Thank you Brian," he said quietly. He stared out of the back window. "I think he was about to... end things."

I nodded, thinking and hurting, drained. I gave myself a cursory check over, my arm had stopped bleeding and apart from that I'd live. I looked like I'd gone a few rounds with Barry McGuiggan on Buckfast, but I'd be all right.

"Please untie me," said Jahn simply.

"Of course," I said absently and walked around the back of him. I reached for his bonds and then stopped myself and stood up again. I walked back around to face him, feeling quite composed and controlled. I knew I had to stay in control a little longer. I fingered out a smoke and lit it.

"What are you doing?" he hissed. "Get me out of here. We need to get this all cleaned up."

I merely blew out a mouthful of smoke and said nothing. I looked into his glazed eyes, now with a renewed fight within them. I was pleased to be alive and not to be the one tied to a chair.

"What were you doing with the van, cutting across me like that?"

"I don't know what you're talking about," he said irritably. "Caskey come on, untie me."

I took another drag.

"Here's another question then," I said, taking my time. "What were you doing here at all?"

He looked up at the ceiling and back to me. "Look… I'm hurt, get me out of this and we'll talk."

I finished my smoke and threw it on the ground; it wouldn't exactly spoil the look of the place. I don't know if it was the nicotine hit, my meds wearing off, or the simple gravity of the situation, but I felt panic creeping in slowly around under my skin. Something also told me not to let this man loose.

"I don't think so, we'll talk now," I said, trying to sound authoritarian. "Either that or I'll run along and call the police, and you can explain things to them."

"You wouldn't want to do that," he said, his voice colder than the recent snow hail.

"And why's that?" I asked, my voice raised. "Because I'm meant to be some kind of patsy? Is that it?"

"No. You've got things wrong."

"Have I? You send me to follow someone and then purposely block me from getting there. Why do that? To put me near to the scene of the crime maybe?"

I lit up another cig and chewed on the end. I was thinking out loud, testing things out, hoping to read some flicker on his face.

"You're the one who just killed a guy Caskey, you don't want to—"

"Shut up," I demanded, turning on my heel and taking a step towards him. I got right up in his face. "Shut up a minute," I said quietly.

I paced about, smoking. What the fuck was going on? I couldn't get my mind to unpack it. I was sure it was there and I was just being slow. My emotions kept flitting about too, somewhere between rage and fear.

"I guess you hadn't wanted things to end with you in this chair, so maybe you were going to kill him and try and put me in the frame?" I said coolly.

His expression was blank, his eyes had reduced to standby.

"You've got it wrong," he said softly, shaking his head.

I began sweating and felt all my new cuts and bruises at once. "Well you don't need to frame me now 'cause I did the job for you... Fuck!" I added, suddenly enraged. His quietness only infuriated me more. I strode across the room and smacked him a backhander across his face. His neck snapped back and a new welt appeared on his cheek. I admit that it felt good, even when he cried out with the shock of it.

"Fuck you Caskey," he said under his breath, looking at the floor.

"No fuck you! And fuck Hertogen!" I shouted. "All this to put me in the frame," I said and spat on the floor. Moving towards him, I met his dull eyes. I knew mine were blazing. I punched him heavily in the stomach and he lurched as much as he could within his bonds. I didn't feel good about it, but I admit I wasn't much in control anymore.

"Well?" I continued, rather weakly. I didn't feel so great about myself at all. I was feeling like a spoilt rich kid, kicking his dog.

"I've got nothing to say," he replied, coughing and wheezing some. "You're crazy, you need help."

"Do I?" I asked, standing over him, my voice faltering. I'm ashamed to say I felt like crying.

I stood over him and looked around the room. I noted that the light was going and the room was taking on a still greyness. My body ached and my mind wished I had made some different choices. I looked over at the wretched heap in the corner that used to be Blakey. I turned back to Jahn. I took my time before sending a right hook hard into his jaw. Some blood spurted out and his eyes looked stunned. My fist throbbed. It took a second one to send him unconscious.

***

I went to the bathroom first. As soon as the buzzing light strip illuminated the mirror and my greying face, panic fully set in. My hands were shaky with nerves. I tried to give myself something to do with another smoke, but I started to cough and then gag. I washed my face and took my blood-stained shirt off. I wanted to get out of there as soon as I could. I looked in the mirror—could have been worse. I wished I was somewhere else, maybe someone else. Maybe I wished I was Billy Chapman. Forcing my body to keep going, I found a bedroom and a clean shirt. I sat down on the sofa, back in the sitting room, across from the two slumped bodies. After a few minutes, I made up my mind what to do, put on my jacket, and was out the door. The resolution at least let me dial back one notch from total panic.

The outside world felt strange and like I had been away from it for many years. It was also fucking freezing. A drizzle came down and a few drips went down my collar. Part of me wanted to just drop down and lie in the gutter. I don't really remember how I found my way to the station and onto the train and then all the way back to Brussels. It's a miracle that I had the wherewithal to do it. I suppose people can do all sorts even when they're sleep walking. I had left Jahn untied, but unconscious, leaving the photograph of Blakey in his wallet instead of mine. I didn't want him dying of thirst or injuries and have that on my conscience too. Besides, I still hadn't decoded exactly what he and Hertogen were guilty of. I also wiped both blades down, and anything else obvious that I had touched. I didn't have much of a plan, mainly that I knew I had to put some distance between me and that place.

When I got into the central station again, I realised my options weren't good. I shouldn't go to my hotel, I probably shouldn't try and leave the country and I definitely shouldn't go to the police. Fuck it, I decided, this had gone too far, too fast. I needed help from somewhere; I was too at risk from all angles. There was no one to trust and I didn't know who might be looking for me soon. I'd go to the embassy.

Chapter Forty-Six

I sat with a cup of coffee, admiring my new watercolour above the fireplace, that I had just finished hanging. It was one of a kind. It was the only piece of art in my home anyhow. Perhaps I was reading too much into things, but the gift seemed a little off and the note pointed. Maybe I was just a sour old buzzard, who saw angles in anything. Or, maybe he had been notified of my asking around about him, maybe John had said something? It certainly wasn't a threat, but was this a hint at a pay-off, reminding me that the case was 'closed?' What I did know, was that McBride was as good a place to start investigating properly as anywhere. He had just made it simple for me. I rang up Stark and went through the bits of information I had gathered and about my recently arrived gift. I could hear him make a few grunts of interest, in between puffing on that pipe of his.

"All right," he said in his gruff, country twang, "we'll keep on going, I appreciate it Chapman. Is there anything you need from me?"

"I'm glad to. Yes, there is actually, can you pull me McBride's full service record and the one for Fotheringay while you're at it?"

"That shouldn't be too hard, yes, but just between you and me, you understand? I could get in quite a bit of bother."

"Loud and clear, thanks. Over and out."

***

The files arrived by first class a few days later, and I took them down to a greasy spoon I frequent around Avoniel. I gobbled up a full 'Ulster,' with extra bacon, and set the unopened package on the empty seat at the table. I drank a second cup of coffee and looked out the window towards the docks up from Sydenham. I was working myself up to it. My mind wondered to Mary and the Causeway. What was she doing right now, I thought? Teaching a class? Walking down at the stones? My mind flitted back to the sheer cliffs and those hexagonal rocks beneath them. Did she still think of me? I pictured a body falling, though I couldn't see it clearly. I shook my head and returned to the small, simple tearoom. There were only a few folks in, some reading the papers, one doing the crossword. One workman in overalls leaned at the coffee bar, dragging on a 'Lucky.' I cast my eyes down to the package and pushed aside the noise of the room and the thoughts of Mary. I dived in.

It took me about an hour to skim through both reports. I paused for just a second and then started at the beginning again, along with my notebook and pen. Before I knew it, it was lunch time and I felt obliged to buy a sandwich and another cup of coffee. I had gone through both reports twice and my little notebook had about a dozen newly filled pages. The hunch looked like it had been worth it. I wasn't much closer on a motive if there even was one to find, but I was closer to something.

Nineteen twenty-nine was the year that interested me. McBride had been based at the barracks in Leicester that year and had been for three previously, having been promoted in 1928 to colour sergeant and to the management of a small company. In May, he requested a transfer home to Belfast, staying at the same rank. He moved home in July and resigned from his post and duty altogether the following November. Fotheringay was originally from Portsmouth and began his military career in Leicester too. He was at the same barracks there as well, that same year. He had started as a lance corporal that January and in June, he also put in for a transfer to stay at the same position, then moving to London that August. Maybe it all meant nothing, or perhaps it mattered a lot.

***

My next move wasn't clear and it took me a few days of false starts to make any progress. I decided to speak to a contact I had at the Belfast News and arranged a meeting for the following Monday. That night I drank a little too much and woke up around three, sweating and my head thumping. I heaved myself downstairs and drank some water, leaning over the kitchen sink. It just hit me. I hadn't been thinking that much about the actual crime scene for a while, but the thought suddenly struck me and the theory presented itself, slotting together in an instant. I scrawled it all down in my notebook, frightened of forgetting any of it the next morning. I went back to bed and surprisingly slept like a bottle drunk baby till eight a.m. At nine, I rang Stark from my office to give him my theory.

"Can you go down to the hotel this morning?"

"Well, I probably could, have you got something?" *he asked, sounding dubious.*

"I might do. It's not about the documents you gave me, I'll come to that later. Would you go back to the function room and take a look at the air grills on the outside wall? At both ends if you would, and inside if you can at all."

"Do you want to tell me what this is all about?"

"I'll be honest with you, I don't want to look daft, I'm playing a hunch. Will you check it out for me?"

"Okay Billy," he said, sounding tired. "I'll ring you back after lunch."

"Thank you, you're a gent," I said and hung up.

***

I waited in my office through lunch and thankfully there wasn't a queue of calls in person, by phone, or otherwise. In fact, there was just one call and that was from the phone company, reminding me to pay my bill. It rang again around twoish.

"Hello, Billy Chapman," I answered on the first ring.

"Okay, there was something."

"Go on," I said, trying not to sound too excited, but I was.

"There are five vents in the wall. They're all about a foot below the high windows. They all looked normal except one. When we had a look inside, it didn't have the middle, thick grill inside. The grill on the outside end in the garden had some fresh scratches on the metal. The inside one had some pretty deep and fresh-looking scores on it too."

"Was it the grill opposite the fireplace?"

"Yeah it was," said Stark slowly. He sounded pleased.

We paused.

"Are you gonna tell me what you're thinking?" he asked.

"Okay, but don't think I'm crazy. How about, a person or persons get Gallagher steaming drunk, just like the autopsy said he was, and sits him in a chair with a Browning by his foot. They wait outside for him to come to, look through the window with only woodland beside them to hide in and in the dark. Once he stands up, they shoot through the vent they've already prepared, and then when they see the first shot wasn't fatal, they shoot again."

I could hear him sucking on that pipe again. It sounded a bit ridiculous said out loud. I half expected him to laugh and hang up.

"Where had he been the previous week? Who would want to do that to him anyway? Would it even be possible?"

"I don't know, it's just a theory," I said, trying not to sound defensive.

"If I took that up the chain, you know what they'd say? Hans Christian Anderson would dismiss it as far-fetched."

"Yeah, but I want to know what you think?"

He went silent, stopping puffing for a moment as well.

"I quite like it," he said.

Chapter Twenty-Seven

Early evening, and folk were out enjoying themselves in the big city, but I certainly wasn't one of them. I sat in the train station, head thrashing, my body still tender. I popped a pill and tapped away at my mobile with a shaky hand. Northern Ireland embassy, right, okay. Google maps... right, *Chaussée d'Etterbeek* 180. I went searching for the tram I needed, my head in a spin. I somehow made it there in a daze. What had I done? Killed a man for one thing and beat up a supposed ally. I was walking the short distance between the tram and embassy, when I doubled over and vomited on the side of the pavement. A couple walked past me and looked me up and down, with open disdain. I steadied myself. "Take it easy Brian," I said out loud, gaining me another look. Was I losing it? Had I got things wrong? All I could do was get somewhere safe. I stopped at a convenience shop, where fortunately the young Belgian behind the counter spoke English. I got some co-codamol, a can of Coke, and new smokes.

***

I stumbled into the building, trying to look together, but failing miserably, I'm certain.

"I need to speak to the ambassador."

The pretty brunette with her hair tied back in a bun looked up from her desk. The normalness and quietness of the office unnerved me further.

"I'm sorry, we are closing in a few minutes and we do not actually have an ambassador here." Her face was genial, but her forehead creased apologetically as she spoke.

I steadied myself and looked around, catching a few office workers peering over at me.

"Are you all right?" she added, the Northern Irish accent almost reassuring me. I wished we were back home, maybe in a pub.

"Well, no, not really. Right," I leaned in and tried to act matter of fact, "I want diplomatic immunity... please."

Her professionalism floundered as she smiled thinly back towards a colleague, with what looked like a shimmer of fear. The other lady looked like she might get involved and ceased her own typing.

"I'm sorry, we can't do that," the girl repeated.

"I'm a Northern Irish citizen," I interrupted, searching my pocket for my passport. I hammered it down on the desk. I noted more looks in my direction and quieted my voice. "I want protection."

She looked at me sympathetically, but nervously, taking a step back from the counter.

"Look, we are not an embassy. This is the Northern Irish Executive office. Northern Ireland does not have an embassy as part of the U.K. We do not have consulate powers," she said, pausing and wrinkling her brow further, like she was questioning if I was hearing her. "You would have to go to the U.K. office for that. That is where the ambassador resides who also represents Northern Ireland."

"Shit," I said hastily and wiped my hand across my face.

I stared down at my passport, my useless passport, my mind racing.

"Is there someone I can call?" she asked uneasily. Several of her colleagues had left their seats and were standing behind her.

"No, no, I'm fine," I said absently. I tried to make myself see a way through.

There was a long silence, though I didn't realise it at the time.

"Are you in some kind of trouble, perhaps I should call the police?" she said gently.

"What?" I demanded, louder than I had intended, plucked abruptly out of my thoughts.

She looked aghast. "I was just thinking, um, I just want to help you," she said weakly.

I had clearly frightened her and I was scared enough for both of us as it was. I shot out the door without a word, leaving an uncomfortable atmosphere in my wake. I stood on the street. It was busy, full of activity, nobody else in the kind of trouble I was in. Fuck! Why had I gone to the wrong one? Of course there would be a central U.K. embassy, shit! I looked down at the passport again in my hand. I turned it over to expose my Irish passport in the back of the plastic wallet. When Brexit started, most N.I. citizens had ordered an Irish one as well, even prods too. The thought struck me. It was the only option I could think of. It was this, or just sit and wait for someone to find me. I could make a run for it, book a flight with my Irish passport. It was worth a go.

***

I set off, a man on a mission. I was balancing on a wire of nerves and it wasn't going too well. I somehow made it out to Charleroi and to the booking desk. I could feel myself coming and going, dipping in and out of complete dread. Part of me just wanted to hand myself in and take whatever was coming from whichever party. I was surprised I'd made it to the airport without a panic attack, or at least a migraine.

"I will just check for you sir," said the girl behind the desk in the crisp blue and white uniform.

I could feel a bead of sweat roll down my brow as I tried to read her face, as she worked on her computer. I was too afraid to draw attention to myself and let it trickle down and fall off.

"Can I see your passport please sir?" she said, looking up.

"Yeah, of course," I said, passing it over, my fingertips leaving the plastic glistening.

She inspected it closely and I tried to look disinterested, and not to show that my heart was beating some kind of three four polyrhythm. She glanced up to look at me and I gave a goofy smile and then tried to frown. Fuck, calm down Caskey, you're frigging this up.

I didn't care much where I could get a flight to at that moment, but there was one for Dublin available in a few hours. I took it, and went out into the smoking area, outside the terminal lounge. I took in heavy lung-fulls, forcing myself to stay together. I hid away in the corner, allowing myself a chance to get ready for the next step. Suddenly my leg started to vibrate. My phone... shit, Hertogen? I took it out and examined the screen. It looked like an N.I. incoming number. I decided I'd answer.

"Hello?" I said gruffly, taking another drag.

"Is that Brian?"

"Who's asking?" I replied sourly.

"Brian Caskey?"

The voice was Northern Irish, male.

"Yeah, that's right," I said, dropping my guard down.

"My name is Doctor Caldwell and—"

"Fuck," I interrupted irritably. "Look, I know I need to book an appointment, I'm out of town on business."

"I'm sorry, I think we are at cross purposes," he said patiently. "I am the doctor for your friend Tim..."

"Tim?" I asked, my mind now a blur.

"Yes, I am very sorry, but I must inform you that Tim has sadly passed away."

I couldn't take in anything more. I hung up.

Chapter Forty-Eight

I arrived at 'The News' at about 9.45, fifteen minutes early in fact. I congratulated myself with a smoke outside, my third of the morning. I was swiftly taken up to A.P. Turner's office.

"Ahh Billy," said Turner warmly, enthusiastically taking my hand, "good to see you."

"And you, it's been a while."

"It has, how have you been?" he asked, offering me a chair.

We chatted and got caught up, having not seen each other for around a year. He was his usual, well-groomed self, confident, but likeable—a journalist in his early forties, still on the up and up. The increase in floor space in his new office and the fashionable, modern looking décor indicated this alone.

"I'll come to the point, I have to ask you two favours," I said with a half-smile that I intended to look endearing.

"Two?" he responded, raising an eyebrow dramatically. "It's been at least a yea. I operate on a one favour a year policy."

"Aww, but you'd stretch to two for me wouldn't you? Anyway, if it leads somewhere I'll give you first notice on the scoop."

"Billy, I'm only kidding pal," he said turning serious. "You know I appreciate everything you did for Laura before and the personal risk you took yourself. My door's always open to you. How can I help?"

"You're a gent," I said. "I appreciate it—and seriously, I'll turn everything over to you first of course.

So, it involves Mervyn McBride, the art dealer—do you know him?"

"Yes, well, I know of him."

"I'm afraid I'm not at liberty to say too much, but I'm looking for any information—personal information. You know the type of thing—how his business is going, any personal troubles, whispers of scandal."

"Okay, sure, I'll see what I can dig up. What's the second thing?"

"It's really a paperwork exercise, the kind of thing a secretary should be able to get for you if you wouldn't mind. I'm looking for any information of interest in the papers around Leicester in 1929. In particular, anything linked to the army barracks there. Again, any scandal, anything noteworthy that year before or in and around the summer."

"Again, that should be fine. No guarantees I'll turn anything up, but I'll try."

"Thank you. One more thing—McBride was there at the time and ideally I'd find something linked to him. Also, relating to both favours, I'd be interested in anything relating to McBride's right hand man. He was at the barracks with him then too—name of Fotheringay."

***

I decided I had worked plenty hard for a few days and took another day off. Man's gotta look after himself. I hopped on a bus from East Belfast, heading out to County Down, but this time the other side, out through Dundonald and Ards. It took about an hour to make it to the sleepy little village of Conlig, which sits in between Bangor and Ards. I was dropped opposite the gothic and impressive old Presbyterian church that dominates the little village. It wasn't even a one-horse town, but it was a one-church town. I crossed the somewhat dilapidated ancient cemetery and climbed the small hill up to the Clandeboye Estate. I meandered through the woodland path, cutting through bramble and leaves, still damp from a mid-morning shower. The walk was brisk, but pleasant. Reaching the end of another path, I took in a deep breath of fresh air and hooked out a cigarette.

After about another half mile, I found my way on to the edge of the golf course. Lord Clandeboye had sold off much of the sprawling estate and one new fixture, then just a few decades old, was an immaculate eighteen-hole course. I had been informed that the monolithic standing stone was on the eighteenth green of the course. I had never seen the appeal of unfit old men whacking a little ball around the countryside, but each to their own. There were a few players out enjoying a game and I tried hard to blend in, albeit with little success. Every glance I received appeared to be a questioning one, asking why this guy in a trench coat was walking through the green, without any clubs. I smiled at each one anyway, for what good it did. What would be the worst that could happen—I'd be asked to leave the course? Oh well.

Anyhow, I continued on and it wasn't long before I was making my way up Hound Hill and onto the eighteenth hole. There it was, the scene of 'The Hound of Ulster.' It's an impressive site if you like that type of thing, and I actually do. The experts say it's prehistoric, but they don't really know why it was placed there. There's hundreds like this throughout the island, a trace of our ancient religions, before we became entrenched in our new ones. That two-metre-tall stone gave me an odd feeling. That tired old rock had somehow taken on many new meanings, perhaps against its will. I heard voices and two players, reaching the end of their battle, began to approach the top of the hill. Shrugging, I gave the stone a last look.

I walked on to the public bar, back at the clubhouse. Inside, I took a whiskey with a little water and had a walk about the traditional old golf pub. The walls were covered *in photographs of past teams, local scenery, and the clubhouse. Beside them was a huge bronze record of every club captain and league table up until that year. One photograph caught my eye. It was an image of the Stone of the Hound from the 1920s. It showed the bottom of it partly buried in a square bank. Maybe that's why it didn't look quite right to me earlier on—the Percy French painting had the bottom buried too. I suppose they must have dug out around it since, maybe to smooth out the green. Pity, I liked it better the other way.*

***

I took the next day off too. Maybe I'd just retire, I thought. I went to visit Mrs. Morris, it's something I do from time to time. Since I had had the unenviable task of telling her how her daughter Laura had died, I'd called maybe three or four times. She seemed pleased to see me, we chatted, enjoyed a sweet sherry together and I was on my way again. She was as elegant and gracious as ever. She told me how the university was naming some prize after Laura and I said I was happy for her. I was *happy for her.*

Chapter Forty-Nine

God knows how I made it back to Belfast. The only way I can describe it is when you drink through the night and gradually become more sober as time goes on. By the time I was stepping off the bus at Great Victoria Street in Belfast, I was feeling more like myself. That and the massive relief and easing off tension, for making it back unmolested. The other half of me was grief-stricken and I felt bad that the relief was the stronger emotion. Poor Tim, my best friend. Maybe he was happier now. At least he had escaped the shit of being alive. No—that's not right Brian, I thought. I kicked some gravel and scolded myself. Walking through the city centre, I felt glad to be home, in the smells and sounds of my city. But it felt different. Nothing would feel right until I had got to the bottom of things, one way or another. I collected my car, dragged myself into the seat and lit up a smoke. My back was still sore from the kicking and my whole body longed for rest and sleep. I switched the ignition and the Black Crowes instantly began to swagger and stomp. I flicked off the player, I wasn't in the mood.

On the drive home, I went over everything in my mind yet again. Did I have to kill the guy? I'm a fucking murderer, but I didn't mean to. I had no choice. Or had I meant to? During my years in the PSNI I had never actually killed anybody. What was Jahn up to and what were Hertogen's orders? Had I got things wrong? Am I unwell? No, no, I wasn't. Had there ever been a connection to the teenager with the wristband? I rubbed at my head, an ache was coming on. Too many questions. Shut up Caskey.

As I turned into my street, I clocked a black Mercedes, further on down the street. I had kind of normalised to the situation since Brussels to some degree, and realised I may have overreacted with the whole embassy thing. Though, then again, I had just killed a potential terrorist! Anyway, I knew things were serious, but I didn't much think I'd be getting caught by the police or anything. Hertogen and his group would want it all hushed up. Now it was them I was more worried about. I peered in the Merc's window as I passed, I couldn't make anyone out inside it or out on the street, but I still had a bad feeling. Fuck. I sped up, took a left, and then pulled over. I child-locked the doors. I took my phone out, switched it off, and took out the battery. Shit—what now? Where the hell should I go? Tim would have been my first choice to go to. There wasn't an obvious second.

***

I drove until my dashboard beeped to tell me that I was low on petrol. I had been more interested in my mirrors, but was fairly sure I wasn't being followed. My brain was flooded, it just needed time to ease and then I could restart it. I didn't want to blow the proverbial gasket. Faces scrolled across my mind's eye: Blakey, Jahn, Hertogen, Tim, Fotheringay. I shook them away.

***

"Billy, sorry, Brian, how are you?" she said, brushing her fringe off her face, trying to sound pleased to see me.

"Sorry Mary, I know it's late," I said, going to check my phone for the time, then remembering it was off.

"No, no, you're fine, it's only coming up to ten," she said, trying to be genial.

She stopped and cast me a look, one that I know she had given me many times before.

"Are you okay?"

"Yeah, I'm grand, well," I faltered, part of me wanted to drop to my knees and have her embrace me and look after me, "I just wanted to chat with you a little bit. Is that all right?"

I saw her note my rucksack on my back and take in properly my dishevelled appearance. She raised an eyebrow. I must have looked like I'd been dragged through a hedge backwards. Actually, it had been worse than that.

"Come in, come in," she said, ushering me inside.

I shuffled in, noticing she wasn't wearing anything on her feet. They were poking out of a pair of old three stripe joggers. Bollox—she was probably about to hit the sack. I went on through, mumbling a few thank-yous. I'd only been in her new place once before. It was a decent end of terrace near the Knock Road in East Belfast. She took me through the unlit hall and into a sitting room and put on the light. She offered me a seat and then hovered by the door. She looked like she was deciding on something.

"Look, I'll be back in a sec. Stick on the telly. Do you want a coffee or something?"

"Please, only if you're having one," I said, taking off my coat. It was cheeky, but I was gasping for one.

"Okay, back in a minute," she said, creasing her forehead. She was looking good. Still had a good figure, even just in an old jumper and tracks.

I put on the TV and flicked on BBC news, half expecting to see my own profile. I heard Mary go upstairs, and then a few creaks on the staircase. After a minute or two, I heard muffled voices and then two sets of steps on the stairs and more creaks. Shit—she had a fella round! Fuck. I could barely recall my marriage, but I instantly felt a weird sense of both jealousy and of being in the way. The front door banged shut and I shuffled uneasily on the sofa. I took in the room and waited. I didn't know what I was going to say, especially not now. The main light was harsh and flooded the small sitting room, its pale blue walls and minimal Ikea-like fittings.

"Sorry about that," she said, opening the door and peering round it. I swear she was blushing, but her eyes were also hard.

"Look Mary," I broke in, "I'm sorry about, well, if I had known you were—"

"It's fine, really," she interrupted, looking mortified, and then she put up a hand to plead for me to say no more. "It wasn't anything important. I'll get you that coffee."

She slipped out and left me to my thoughts. I almost began to laugh out loud, it must have been nerves or something. Though, God was certainly having a good laugh at my expense that last week. I opened up my bag and leafed through it, mostly to give myself something to do. I did want to check what I had remembered though, considering I had crashed into my hotel room and flew out again on the way to the airport. If I had drunk myself sober, then this was now the worst hangover of all bloody time.

She returned with our coffees, a pleasant aroma accompanied the steam piping out of the mugs. She sat across from me on a red and white striped chair. A room of red, white, and blue. You can take the girl out of Ballybeen, but... anyway.

"So, what brings you here Brian?" she said, still trying to be breezy, but with less effort.

I rubbed a hand over my face. I was busting for a smoke, but I knew that'd be met with disapproval.

"I don't know where to start. I suppose I just wanted someone to talk to. I'm sorry, I know I shouldn't be coming to you. Not like this."

"No," she said with a softness, "of course you can."

She stopped and gestured to the door. "Don't worry about that, it's nothing really. I've been worried about you recently. Anyway, are you okay?"

"I've been better," I replied and eased back into the sofa. "I've got a bit of sad news for a start, Tim passed away."

"I know," she said nodding. "It's very sad. I liked him a lot."

"Oh," I said. "Who told you?"

"Brian, I've been trying to get in touch with you for days," she said, her voice almost shrill.

She stood up and paced about, and then sat back down again.

"Okay Brian, it's like this, I'm here for you, but I can't do this every time if you're not going to help yourself."

My mind faltered, I didn't know where she was going with this at all, I was still trying to decide how much I wanted to tell her of the last few days.

"What do you mean, what are you talking about?" I said, tetchily.

"It was your doctor who told me love, they're all worried about you."

"What the fuck?" I said irritably. "Sorry, but what are you going on about, I'm fine."

I swear I thought my head was actually going to explode. Like for real, full fucking 'Scanners.'

"Are you?" she barked and stood up again and crossed to the window, fiddling with the blinds.

"Yes, I really am," I said and tried to look a bit more together than I was.

"Look at the state of you," she shouted. I saw tears in her eyes as she faced the window again.

"I'm fine."

"I told you I was worried about you," she said still standing, and now gesturing heavily with her right hand. "Then your doctors are worried about you too, especially after your best friend dying. Then nobody can find you or talk to you, or check you're okay. I knew you were taking too much on."

"Fucksake," I said through my teeth to the ground, and then I stood up shouting. "There's nothing wrong with me. Frigsake! It'd be easier if you lot all pissed off."

"Then why come here?" she shouted back. "You're fine?" she added sarcastically. "You turn up at my house out of nowhere, nobody's spoken to you for days, you miss your appointments, you come here, bag in hand and looking like an extra in *One Flew Over the Cuckoo's Nest*."

She stopped and calmed, stepping closer to the blinds again, and then looked through them this time, when she moved them, fidgeting. I watched her, trying to calm down. If I really started shouting, I doubted I could have stopped. Then something struck me and a new alarm began sounding off in the mess of my head.

"What have you done?" I asked pointedly.

She ignored me, still looking outside.

"Who have you called Mary?" I asked louder.

"Okay!" she said, spinning around. "Fuck!"

She sat back down and took a sip of her drink.

She shook her head and shrugged. "I had to ring them Brian, after last time... Knockbracken. Okay? I rang Knockbracken."

"For God's sake," I said, just managing to control the rage, yet absently clenching my hands into fists. I bent over and zipped up my bag, and flung it over my shoulder as I headed to the door.

She moved in front of me, her eyes pleading.

"Brian, please don't do this to me again, please don't leave."

"There's nothing wrong with me, all right, look, there is some shit going on, but mentally, I'm doing all right."

She shook her head again. "You don't know what you're saying, you're confused again."

"I'm not," I said sharply, my tired throat cracking.
I paused and looked her in the eye.

"I'm honestly fine. I promise you," I said, gentler.

I turned and started to walk down the path. Mary shook her head and hugged herself against the door frame.

When I got to the gate I smiled and shouted, "Look, we'll just have to agree to disagree—that's what the voices in my head say to each other anyway."

***

After around an hour of driving, I guessed I'd better choose one direction or another. I found myself on the road to Bangor again, speeding along the Sydenham Bypass. This was where it had all begun—starting as just a bit of tailing, feeling good about myself, working on a new novel—that all seemed like a lifetime ago. It was close to half ten when I slowed to thirty and drove through the town centre. My head was fried and I needed somewhere to rest. I couldn't go home, I didn't like the look of that Merc outside. It wouldn't be great if the Mental Health Services were after me, though I didn't think they'd have enough to go on to actually section me. Not this time anyway. Fuck! Where had it all gone wrong? And what about poor Tim? I'd miss him. I knew that once I had some peace after this business was all done with, then I'd feel a keen loss. He was my buddy and had been for years. Maybe he would be at peace at least.

"Yeah, they must have double booked, I don't trust these computer bookings sometimes," I said to the man as he led me up the stairs. I had just cruised along Princetown Avenue, a few streets out of the town centre. The Shelleven was showing a vacancy sign and its lights were still on. Princetown is full of guesthouses. During The Troubles, we used to put up officers from England in places there all the time. Obviously we thought the IRA wouldn't have travelled as far as the bucket and spade town for executions.

"Thanks," I said, after he opened up my room. "Would it be too late for a drink?" I asked, chancing my arm.

I felt my luck was on the turn, finding a decent B and B for a good price and one with a licence. Half an hour later and I was sitting on my fresh bed, stretching out, whiskey in hand, with the Politics Show on in the background. There was something comforting about me locked in the little cocoon, with no one knowing where I was. I actually felt I could breathe normally for a change. Maybe this is what drove me to think, "*Fuck it*," and put my battery back in my phone and switch it on. I knew I couldn't hide forever. I popped one of my pills, sat back, and listened to the conversation of buzzes and beeps coming out of my phone. I waited for five minutes to be sure it had stopped. I felt tense picking it up again.

I checked the emails first, a few from my publisher, nothing urgent, one from the vet. Crap! I'd have to check on Buzzo, he'd be sure to be low on food—bollox. I ignored the Facebook updates, it had been boring recently anyway. I already knew that nobody should have voted for Trump or Brexit, people didn't need to keep finding new ways of telling me. Messages were thin on the ground, probably on account of me not really having many friends. But hey. There were some pleading ones from Mary to get in touch. Some were from before we met and one after. I felt bad as I deleted them one by one.

I set it down and sipped my drink, trying to concentrate on the TV. I needed some head space. About half an hour later and the theme from Columbo began to blast out, signalling an incoming call. I snatched up the phone and noted that the number was withheld. It could be yet another PPI call or fake Microsoft or Nigerian prince, but this time I thought probably not.

"Hello?"

"Hello Brian."

Hertogen's accent and manner were distinct.

"You're a shit Hertogen," I said coldly, sitting up, with my back resting against the wall.

He blew out air. It sounded like he was smoking.

"That is not most friendly. Nor is beating an already beaten and bound man unconscious," he said in a rebuking tone.

"I know your game. I get that it was a frame, I just managed to get out of it, that's all."

I felt flushed and I could hear the panic in my voice, I needed to settle myself.

He sighed. "Mr. Caskey, we must meet to discuss things."

I stood up, raising my voice. "I have to do exactly nothing for you, you pompous fucker. And, if you try and threaten me about Brussels, I'll be telling the authorities all about you and your operations."

"This really won't do," he said calmly, but like a formal diner whose medium steak had arrived well done. "I can come to you at your guest house in Bangor if that is easier?"

I actually shivered. I said nothing, chewing my lip.

"Or, at Mary's, if you plan on returning there," he pressed.

"Leave her the fuck out of this," I said almost screaming. I looked towards my bedroom door, remembering where I was, and lowered my voice. "I want nothing more to do with you. If I have to admit to what happened, then fine. It was self-defence and you are the one up to your neck in shite."

"Mr. Caskey, there really is no need for such animosity. I am the one wronged here and poor Jahn. I am willing to be forgiving, but my patience will not last indefinitely." He paused and seemed to take a drag on a cigarette. "I have not lied to you at any point, nor done you any harm. It must be fairly obvious that things did not go as I or anyone else planned in Brussels."

"Yeah, but you fucking had me followed and set me up. The plan was obviously for Jahn to kill Blakey and pin it on me."

"That most certainly was not the plan," he said firmly. "However, I will concede that in my line of work, you must prepare for... how you say, eventualities."

"Yeah, like pinning a murder rap on me."

"I admit that it was an outcome I could envision. As I said, I have never lied to you Mr. Caskey, and I am not doing so now. It was not the strategy I had chosen. It would be foolish for me to discuss all of my confidential knowledge and all of the possible outcomes I have thought through."

"But you would have been happy to sell me out?" I said, trying to sound more reasonable.

"I would have not been happy," he said irritably. "You must understand and see the bigger picture here. I admit that at times I have had to choose the lesser of two evils. We are dealing with international terrorists and without full government support. I primarily hired you for your skill, your association already with people in this network, but yes... if I needed to, would I protect the entire operation and all of the undercover agents, by arranging it to look like an ex-policeman with personal struggles working alone? Yes, of course I would."

I didn't know what to say. At least he was being honest I supposed, or partly. He certainly wasn't exactly wooing me. I was still mightily pissed off, but I begrudgingly understood better.

"All the same, I've got nothing more to meet with you about. Stay away from me and Mary. If you don't, I'll spill my guts and take you down with me."

"No, Mr. Caskey," he rasped. "This is where things are at. I have been reasonable. I have tried to explain my predicament fairly. If you try and make any waves for me, you know that I can arrange a tsunami for you."

He paused, and I could hear anger beneath his always controlled tone. "You can prove the total of nothing. You do not know my real name, you have no contact details for me, you know nothing. Text messages and phone records can all be erased. There is no CCTV footage from any of the times we met. There are no waiters paid enough to say they saw us together, after some pressure is applied." He paused again and sounded as if he had just finished reading a passage as part of a sermon. "So, I need to meet with you tomorrow urgently. This will happen and it can be done with your cooperation or without it. Do not test me."

I unscrewed my face and bit on my lip. I knew I was beaten, all ways round. There was nothing for it, but to meet with him and play it from there. He was my only way out of all of this.

"Fine, tomorrow's Saturday and there's a match on at the Oval at three," I said, trying not to sound too beaten down. "The Milk Bar café in the ground will be open earlier. I'll see you inside at two. Feel free to enjoy some top European football afterwards."

"I will see you then. I cannot promise to stay for the match. Please do not do anything stupid before then, I will know if you do anyhow. Enjoy your guesthouse."

There was a click when he hung up. I went outside and smoked my brains out. The dice were cast and there was nothing I could do about it. I had to just get through it and hope that I could make it through. I spent most of the rest of the night on my laptop with Billy Chapman.

Chapter Fifty

The next few days were quiet and I did a fair amount of drinking, that both my wallet and liver could ill afford. One night I tried to be social and headed out to The Crown. I just ended up sitting at the bar by myself and drinking too much local whiskey. The case was aggravating me and had gotten under my skin. As I sat there, drinking and smoking, my mind flitted back to the war—those terrible days, but also purposeful. Yes, I was ultimately injured and experienced some terrible stuff, but my time out there wasn't something I regretted. I knew what my role was and someone was always there to tell me if I needed it. Who tells you how to get on in life out here? I was sitting in my office when the call came through. It was Saturday morning and I had been considering trekking up to Distillery to see the Glens. It wasn't the same as going to the Oval, but it was the best for now.

"Well, I can tell that this Fotheringay is a funny character."

"Oh," I said. We were a few minutes into our conversation, when A.P. Turner began to share what he had managed to find out so far.

"Yes, I spoke to a couple of sources who know him and McBride, and have dealings in the art world. Most speak respectfully about McBride, but Fotheringay appears to ruffle people up the wrong way. Most I've talked with don't really care for him. His background is that he only made it to corporal after his few years in the army, and that seems to be through family connections more than anything else. Still though, he is said to convey an arrogance, and likes to pontificate about his army days."

"I've spent some time with him, the arrogant thing, yeah I get it."

"McBride is still a big player in the art world, but apparently has lost it a bit recently, possibly in part to do with bringing Fotheringay on board. He's essentially a hired help, but sometimes acts a bit like he's running the show."

"That's interesting, thank you. I appreciate it. Did you find anything to do with Leicester?"

"They didn't manage to find anything involving those two by name. There hadn't been anything really in the press involving the barracks until the May and there was something pretty big."

"Go on," I said eagerly.

"A man, name of Richard Robinson, was a young private at the time. He was on a day's leave and attended a rally in Leicester centre, one Wednesday night. He was found dead early the next morning, out on a pathway in Bradgate Country Park. He had been shot in the head, his service weapon on the ground beside him. The verdict was released swiftly as a suicide. According to the press at the time, no obvious reason was found for his sudden demise. He was an enthusiastic young man, courting a local girl, and had spent much of his free time from barracks at liberal political rallies."

I chewed on it for a second before speaking.

"I really appreciate your help. That's very useful. I think there might be something there."

"I'm glad. Can you tell me anything about what angle you're working on?"

"I'm sorry, I really can't. I've got a very fussy client, but as soon as things get wrapped up, you'll be first to know."

"I understand Billy, good luck with it."

I took the first train out to Newcastle the next morning. That night though, I put on my best suit and headed out for drinks in Belfast. I wasn't meeting anyone, but I felt good. I just wanted to go out. I had that nervous anticipation involved when a case started to crack just a little bit. I had a few in White's and stumbled upon a concert in the Ulster Hall. It was a free night of gospel music with some touring acts from the States. It was to raise money for rebuilding some of the war-damaged churches in South Belfast.

I went on in and listened to a couple of average acts. Gospel isn't exactly my first choice, I like blues music and a little swing. Then five singers came on, black and all of about eighteen. I had only seen about two coloured people in my life before that and here were five of them together. They were billed as 'The Five Blind Boys of Alabama' and they were incredible. The crowd really took to it right away and the atmosphere was like no church I had ever been to. I've never been one much for religion and all that good feeling, but that night I could see the appeal of it.

***

I arrived before lunch time and walked straight through Newcastle town, a light rain soaking my jacket some. I had arranged to call again on Gallagher's cousin, Frances McParland. The kindly, slightly gruff country lady offered me tea and shortbread. They were both lovely.

I soon came to the point and said, "I was hoping you could tell me something about his past, perhaps even before he met his future wife?"

She sipped her tea and put her half-eaten shortbread down on her Willow pattern saucer.

"So you still think there is something to investigate?"

"I am afraid so Mrs. McParland. I am not convinced that your cousin took his own life, as terrible as that would also be."

She gave me a hard look and then softened.

"I don't know what to think," she said sombrely. "But, I would like to know the truth."

"That's what I want too, and any help from you might well get us closer to it."

"Okay, let me think, well, in the 1920s and '30s, he was mostly doing odd jobs around the town, a bit of work here and there, a little farming too. In the late twenties he lived in England for a little while and then moved back and started working in bars and hotels."

"Oh," I said, "I hadn't realised he had lived out of the country for a time."

"Yes, he had been involved in some, well it's not fashionable now," she added somewhat sheepishly, "rather right-wing politics. He had joined a few groups here and wanted to be part of the growing movement on the mainland. This was all around the time of 'The Crash' and right-wing politics was really quite common," she said stopping. "Do you think this might be relevant?"

"Yeah, I think it could be. What did his work over there involve?"

"I think it was all sorts, there wouldn't have been much money from it, just board and that, but he had a lot of responsibilities I think in a small group. I suppose he did a lot of recruiting and spreading the word, things like that."

"Do you know whereabouts in England he was living?"

"It was around Leicester I think."

***

My *next appointment had been already made the previous day through Mr. McBride's secretary. When she had called me back, she had said that he would gladly meet me briefly at midday at the Slieve Donard. When I came in through the large doors and into the grand reception, it was in fact Fotheringay who greeted me.*

"Mr. Chapman," he said simply and crisply. He looked as prim and supercilious as ever.

"Fotheringay. I was expecting Mr. McBride," I stated directly.

He had dialled back his warmth towards me, but then returned it one notch.

"Yes, I'm afraid something has come up, but I can speak with you in his place for a short time."

"Let's get a drink then," I said, leading the way to the bar.

We both ordered, him a glass of red and me a pint of stout. We retired to a quiet window seat at the back of the lounge. He lit up a cigarette, mustn't have been in the mood for a cigar. I lit one too and raised my eyes to meet his stare.

"I really do not understand what there is still to discuss," he started squarely, "but we are willing to try and wrap this all up finally. Did you receive the painting?"

"Yes, I did, I will thank Mr. McBride personally."

His face flickered, an impatient grimace passing over it.

"As I said, he is very busy and I am here in his place to close our business. Mr. McBride will not be meeting you in addition. You have been paid already of course and we do not wish you to investigate any further, thank you."

"I would have thought that you both would have wanted to get to the truth of the death."

"But we have," he said, abruptly flicking the ash off the end of his mostly smoked cigarette. He put it out and lit up another.

"I do not think we have. Gallagher didn't kill himself, I never believed he had."

"But that is preposterous, the police are satisfied, as are the courts."

"Well I'm not," I said with a shrug and let that hang there. "As I said, it was no suicide. He was intoxicated, left with a gun beside him and shot through an air vent by a second gun."

I noted panic, and then anger on his face. "Mr. Chapman, you really must leave this," he said breathily. "You are in danger of becoming quite ridiculous."

I continued on, calmly and assuredly.

"It makes better sense if first you reject the notion that it was Gallagher who carried out the initial robbery. This was merely a ruse to help with the orchestration of murdering him."

"Mr. Chapman," were the only words he softly said, shaking his head and looking down at the table. But I could tell he was thinking hard.

"It was a set up from the get go, he was to be silenced. It was nothing to do with the pictures."

"Can I just remind you that we employed you in this matter, and we were trying to save any harm to Mr. Gallagher, I say this before you get any more funny ideas."

"Ideas like what?" I said somewhat insolently, and he took it that way, a flare of frustration again crossing his lips. He dialled back any remaining warmth further.

"Well, by what you say and your tone and manner, I fear you see myself or Mr. McBride involved in some kind of ludicrous conspiracy."

"So there's nothing new you would like to share?" I asked tonelessly.

He sucked on his cigarette and took a long, slow drink. I pulled my best innocuous face and lit up another smoke too, enjoying myself.

"Of course not," he said slowly and with some effort.

"Let me ask you something else then," I said dryly. "Do you recall a Richard Robinson?"

He suddenly became very still and attentive. Then he tried to be nonchalant. "I don't believe so, no. I meet a lot of people."

"Just have a think," I added, feeling like I was holding three jacks and the river card was still to show. "I think he would be someone you would remember."

He made a show of trying to recall the name, looking up at the cornicing in the ceiling and everything.

"No, it rings no bell," he said.

I licked my lips. "You were stationed in Leicester army barracks, under the command of Mr. McBride, back in 1929."

I stopped and looked at him; somewhere in the back of those double-glazed eyes, there was fear. Cold, hard fear, no doubt about it.

"While there, a colleague of yours, this Richard Robinson, died. It was supposedly suicide as well, but as with Gallagher, I don't think so."

"You are a meddler Mr. Chapman," he said bitterly and through his teeth, and I had the feeling that I was glimpsing the real Fotheringay for the first time. "I do not know what you expect to get out of this, but I demand that you stop. I will view any further intrusion on our private lives as continuing harassment. I will contact the police myself in this matter if needs be. I have many influential friends."

I held my own and continued unfazed. "I find it a strange reaction to become quite threatening when I merely ask you if you remember a colleague of yours who died in a well reported incident. You still don't remember him?"

He held my stare as if trying to make up his mind. He knew he was holding nothing and it was time to leave the table.

"I do not have to answer any of your questions and have been more than patient," he said in an irate whisper.

"This meeting is over and neither of us will be meeting with you any further."

I offered him my widest smile and said, "Well last time I checked, you and Mr. McBride are not the same person. You're not even his senior. He's your boss. I wanted to speak to the organ grinder and all I got was the monkey."

He stood up sharply and I thought he had lost it altogether. He gathered himself and checked around before leaning in to me, saying, "You're playing a dangerous game. You're out of your league here. Besides, you have nothing."

"You should have said you remembered him," I replied, and necked the last of my drink. I stood up and brushed past him.

"Be seeing you," I said.

Chapter Fifty-One

I chose the Conlig route on my way back to Belfast the next morning. As I went along the carriageway, I looked out towards the Clandeboye Estate and where Percy's stone would be sticking out of the ground there. In that moment, I wished that my job was just writing and not getting myself into these scrapes. It wasn't and it was my own fault for getting tied up in things. I had no desire to be the Hound of Ulster, but it didn't really matter what I wanted anymore. All I could do was press on. I was just a vessel, moving with the tide.

There had been an email informing me of Tim's funeral for that morning at Roselawn. It's the only crematorium in the province and provides an unfortunate kind of factory line of half hour slots. I sat in the carpark, a thin drizzle rinsing some of the dirt off my old Ford. After twenty minutes or so, I watched as they carried him in. I recognised a few of his family. I had no interest in going inside, it certainly would make no odds to Tim. When they were all inside, I switched the ignition and pulled the handbrake off.

I felt a melancholy for Tim and yes for myself. I didn't care much about Hertogen or his setup. I certainly didn't really give a fuck about the guy who I killed in Brussels. I knew I had had no choice and my only reason for going in that house in the first place was to save someone I thought innocent. I should have known better than anyone—nobody's innocent. It's a funny life and I started to dwell on it. How strange life is, these stories that make up our existence. What was my story before Knockbracken? What about when I was a so-called family man? If you were to splice my story from after the

Causeway and up until I met Hertogen, it wouldn't be bad. You'd have to edit a much smaller part of my life if you wanted it to be a happy story.

***

I drove the final stretch to East Belfast and parked my car along Dee Street. Before that, I nipped in home to feed the cat and check no spies were hanging about my gaff. All was clear. I went to a greasy spoon off Dee Street for a fry at lunch time and sat with a second cup of coffee, calming my nerves as best I could. Many times I had sat there, readying before a big game against 'The Blues.' This meeting at the Oval had much more serious consequences. I didn't have much of a game plan myself, I'd have to wait and see what Hertogen had to say. Besides, it appeared he was holding all the cards. As I sat over my coffee, out of nowhere that image of Sean came into my head. Sean, the football, East Belfast. Sean, my son. But I didn't remember him. Not really. He drifted off again, back into the murkiness of my memories and who I used to be.

***

"Tenner please."

"Cheers," I said absently, as I brushed through the revolving turnstile. I supposed I wouldn't be claiming expenses any longer. There were smokers loitering around the yard inside the Oval and some folk selling merchandise and programs. I lit up a smoke and ambled over to a seller, thinking I'd get a programme to help remember the day. I've always been a fan of irony.

"Thee fifty please mate," said the burly seller in a broad accent.

"I hope we don't get robbed on the pitch as well today," I said with a wink, handing over the money. I finished the smoke and went for a leak in the old toilet block off to the side. I came back out and hacked my way through another smoke. It was a sunny day and it didn't do the ground any favours; not much looked changed since it was rebuilt after the war. At quarter to two, I bought a coffee in the milk bar and turned around to find the best table for our meet. It looked a bit like a workingman's club from the eighties and that's probably when it was last decorated. I was taken aback to see Hertogen already seated in a small booth in the corner. I hadn't spotted him when I went in. His choice of crisp suit was sitting immaculate as ever, though he didn't exactly blend in. A few tables to the left was Jahn, one black coffee and two black eyes. Jahn looked away towards the door, but Hertogen's eyes traced my movements as I traversed the crowd beginning to form, all dressed in green, black, and red. It wouldn't be as packed as it could be as we were only playing dirty old Ards.

"Welcome to the home of football," I said wryly, taking a seat.

"Thank you," he said. "Thank you for coming."

"I didn't have much choice."

"No," he said vaguely.

"What do you want Hertogen?" I asked, bending over the table, trying to look as intimidating as I could.

"I need you to do one last thing."

"I don't think so."

He leaned back in his chair. "I said I need you to, it is not a request."

I took out my lighter and began to fidget with it. I had nothing to add, all I could do was listen.

"I am a forgiving person, a reasonable man. Jahn over there is not so. I want you to do this last thing and then that is it. Then I go away, Jahn goes away, and everything goes away."

I leaned in further. "Well Jahn has a fucking bad memory then, because I saved his fucking life and saved him from a brutal torture that he was about to get."

"Perhaps the beating you gave him to the head affected his memory," he responded dryly.

"Look, here is the money you were owed, plus a large amount extra," he said, pushing an envelope under the table. I reluctantly closed my fingers around it and shoved it into my inside jacket pocket. I'd prefer to have taken a bung from Stark.

"What is it you want me to do? Let me make this clear though first, I'm not walking into another fucking trap. You tell me everything and make sure I believe you. Maybe I'll do what you want. That had better be it though Hertogen," I said firmly, holding his stare.

His eyes held firm, and then he looked away for a moment and back to me, his face less taut than it had been. The noise increased around us as the build up to the match increased. The roll call of players could also be heard faintly from the tannoy in the background.

"As I said last night, I have not lied to you, I am just not able to always tell you everything. I take no pleasure in this aspect of the work, it is though a necessity."

He took a sip of his coffee and made a face, returned his cup to the table and pushed it to the side. I understood that at least, the coffee was indeed weak as piss.

"I need you to conduct some urgent surveillance and quite possibly an intervention. It will be tomorrow." He looked around at the room, now heaving and getting noisy. "Can we walk?"

"Okay, sure."

We walked along the home terrace behind the goals, the sun beating down on our backs, casting a shadow through the nets. Not many supporters had taken their spots yet. On a quiet match day, most would probably choose the stand anyway. Jahn walked a few paces behind us both, on his phone, or at least pretending to be.

"I will be quite frank with you Mr. Caskey. You are aware that we have been gaining intelligence on a terrorist cell and that this cell has been supported by persons in Northern Ireland. The unfortunate incident in Brussels appears to have sped up the initiative of this group. New information has informed us that they are quite undeterred by this. You should know that we took care of everything and as far as they are concerned, Blakey is just missing. Of course, they will assume he is either dead or has given up information, or perhaps both. It appears that they can afford to be reasonably confident, as he did not know the full details of their planned operations."

He stopped to see if I was following it all.

"Go on," I said, looking out at the pitch where both teams were warming up, doing stretches and practicing set pieces.

"I trust that you will keep everything I tell you confidential. You may not feel you owe anything to us, but a great many lives depend on it."

"Fine," I said. I was still playing tough, but of course it mattered to me. I may have been a washed-up cop who never lasted long in the force, with mental health problems, but. Well, let's leave it at, it mattered to me.

He swallowed and we stopped walking, just behind the nets. He actually looked nervous. For the first time, he looked like a real person to me.

"We have intelligence that a bomb will be planted tomorrow in Belfast and that it will be set to go off at some point during the next week. Simultaneously, bombs will be planted in other cities, all set to detonate at the same time."

He stopped and stared at me, looking for a reaction and I tried not to give him one, but I couldn't help it.

"What other cities?" I asked.

"Their plan is not to hit the most major cities, London, Edinburgh, and so on. It is vastly more difficult to strike a higher profile city or big event. We have not confirmed it all completely, but it seems they want to make a large impact by hitting somewhere in each country at once instead, we think Belfast, Southampton, Sterling, and Holyhead."

"Fuck," I said, giving up on trying to hide my feelings.

A breeze blew through the ground and we shivered in tandem.

"As you can see, there is a great deal at stake, a great deal."

"What's your plan for tomorrow?"

"There are a number of suspects and there may well be a deliberate decoy or two also. They know that they are ahead of us, but careful just the same. You are to be part of the surveillance team. If you believe your target is planting a device, then you must use the walkie talkie you'll be given to request back up. We do not want any rash heroics in the middle of the city."

I stopped, watching the players go back down the tunnel, prior to the final pitch inspection. I turned to Hertogen, and stopped, square on.

"I still don't fully get why you want me."

He looked up at some Ards fans taking their lonely seats across the way. Two team flags rippled against the metal rails.

"As I have said before, we are a small operation. We are not government sanctioned."

"Well, what about that then, why aren't you? Fucksake! Surely this is something they'd want to know about?"

He shook his head and slipped his hands into his pockets.

"If only it were that simple. You do not understand Brian. There are many departments in my country. There are many countries in Europe. There are many allegiances, many enemies, at home and abroad. There are also many personal interests. You must only look at the various coups around the world, Trump, Brexit, Russia's displays of strength, military actions in Korea. They all link. There are never only two sides. There are more angles than there are blades of grass on this pitch. That is why at the end of this, if we are completely successful, there will be no noise, no headlines, no interviews. You will have had nothing to do with it. I will pass it on quickly to others very delicately and I will have had nothing to do with it either. We want to take them alive and then it will be someone else's job to glean information from them regarding the other planned attacks. That is the best outcome." He stopped and looked at me with heavy eyes and I could see strain on every inch of his face. "Will you help us?"

I rolled my eyes. "I can't say no anyway and I still know that I'll be your patsy if it comes to it, but yeah, I'm in."

"Thank you Mr. Caskey," he said with a warmth that may even have been half real. "When you return to your car, in the glove box you will find the walkie talkie I mentioned and a small handgun."

Chapter Fifty-Two

I arrived at the police station with no appointment and I hadn't even told Stark that I was travelling down yet. Unfortunately he wasn't in.

"He may be back before the end of the day," the young officer told me from behind the desk of the little station. "Would you like to leave a message?"

I pushed a sealed envelope across the desk.

"I have some information that I was to pass on to him, the name's Billy Chapman."

"Yes, I've heard the name, I can see he gets it once he's back in. Like I said, might not be 'till tomorrow, but I can leave it for him on his desk."

"Okay, thanks," I said. "Would you have pen and paper, I'd like to leave him a note and where he can find me later if he wants to meet up. It doesn't matter if it's late."

"Certainly," he said and passed them both across the desk.

I wrote a few lines and folded over the paper. Pulling the envelope back, I placed it inside and pushed it back to him.

"Thanks for your help," I said and went out into the afternoon, a cool early frost not far away. I returned to the Donard, and booked a room with the receptionist. It wasn't exactly like Jesus on Palm Sunday. Parsons was standing by the door of his office at the back and peered over his glasses at me. He didn't manage a warm greeting or even a smile, and went back inside his office. It seemed nobody was pleased to see me. Oh well, I wasn't in this game for the social aspect. I spent the early evening in my room, smoking and running things over in my mind. An

unforgiving rain was on outside and the night had turned black. I booked a local taxi to pick me up at eight and got it to leave me a street away from McBride's house. It hadn't been difficult to find out where he lived, but there was no guarantee he'd be home, or even in town. I had a feeling though that I'd catch up with him that night sooner or later.

Chapter Fifty-Three

After Hertogen had briefed me further, the teams came on to a thin cheer and soon he was gone. I stayed to watch most of the first half. It was shit and I wasn't really in the frame of mind for it anyway. As I crossed the yard, there was the smell of chips and cigarettes and a few people were milling about. They must have reckoned it was shit too. Some had maybe left early to go for a slash or queue for food and drinks. The sun was still hot enough and it made me blink. My head hurt and I was dog tired. I looked up at the murals of players from the past and I thought about Billy Chapman and his adventures, and his own wanders around the Oval. He wasn't real, but maybe he was my small way of making a link with the past, maybe it's what we all try and do. That rose-tinted glasses thing—'Things were better in my day.' Well in fairness, in the '40s there were a shit load of bombs dropping, and rationing, and polio, so maybe not that much better. In saying that, the Glentoran team was better than the shite I had just been watching. It was a Wizard of Oz team, as they say. No courage, no brains, no heart.

Dee Street was quiet when I got back to my car. As I settled into my seat, I flipped open the glove compartment discreetly, and sure enough they both were there. I fully expected them to be, no sign of entry either. I don't know the make of the walkie talkie, but the gun was a Glock 17. I closed the compartment door and checked my phone. There was another missed call from Mary and a few more texts. I felt shitty about things, but there wasn't much I could do about it all. Not yet.

I decided I didn't want to go home again for the night and that Buzzo had enough food to do him. Carpe that diem—I may as well spend some of that bloody money, I thought. I set off for the Crawfordsburn Inn, figuring I'd treat myself if they had a room free. I'd stay the night and head straight to the job from there.

As I crossed onto the duel carriageway, I thought through what Hertogen had told me. My job would be to tail Regan again. I was to keep them regularly updated and if I needed assistance, someone could be there within twenty minutes. That was all right as far as it went, but I knew that any kind of shit might go down. Traffic was light and as I passed the Oval on the other side of the ground, I heard a cheer go up. I stuck on Radio Ulster, only to be informed that Ards had just scored twice. Jesus, they'd been in the second division up to the year before.

I turned off the main road before Crawfordsburn and went a bit further down to the outskirts of Bangor. I fancied some chips and hadn't been to 'Colin's' in years. I was pleased to see familiar old faces and the distinct smell of well made, proper local chip shop chips. In total, I got myself a chicken pie, chips, and beans, with a can of full fat Coke. I drove down to the seafront and devoured them there. There's something great about eating chips in the car by the sea, just as it's getting cold. I had a sense of the inevitable upon me, things would change and it was coming soon.

***

I was parked outside the hotel within the quarter hour. The thatched roof looked newer than the 1600s, which is when I'm led to believe it first went up. The whole building looked well in the late afternoon sun. I had never stayed in the infamous hotel before, but had had a few meals there and a lot more drinks. Van the Man is meant to be a frequenter, but I never once had stumbled into him.

There was no problem getting a room and I actually felt pretty relaxed, sitting by the open fire in the old snug, downing a few shorts. I smoked nearly two packs that day too. If the next day was to all go tits up, at least I'd made a dent into the envelope of money. I let my mind wander, drift about, I let it off the leash. It was something I generally tried to avoid, because I could never be sure it would return. Hotels can let you do that. I thought about Tim, poor sod. I probably could have been a better friend. No point in thinking about that now. Poor Mary—a child dead and a fuck up of an ex-husband. I drifted back to the room and the sweet smell of peat and well-cooked meals.

The lounge was fairly quiet, and at around eight I nipped to my room for my laptop and brought it back downstairs and got comfy. The fire had just been stoked and I ordered myself a hot whiskey, with extra lemon and cloves. If I didn't spoil myself, no one else was going to.

I googled about the Brussels embassy in Belfast myself and could find nothing of importance. The same went for 'Hertogen,' where I found nothing much at all. I searched for recent news about a murder in Brussels and found quite a few. None of them were committed by me though. I got another hot toddy and tried one last search.

This time I looked for terrorist groups in Northern Ireland. Stupidly I got a gazillion hits about The Troubles. I followed it up, looking for things like 'Islamic extremism in Northern Ireland.' There wasn't much that came up and certainly I had never seen much local news relating to it. One thing I found was about a local man who had been in jail already and then apparently radicalised. Seemingly, he fancied making an assassination attempt on Prince Harry. He only got as far as making a few notes and then actually handed himself in. They then dutifully put him away again. And there's me thinking I'm a nut! It made me feel better anyway.

I locked myself in my room for much of the night, my mind taking a time out from the real world, and spending some more time in the 1940s. I sat there and wrote and wrote and wrote. I'd be in good company, according to the hotel guide book, so too did C.S Lewis, Jonathan Swift, and Charles Dickens.

Chapter Fifty-Four

*T*hankfully the rain had broken into a light drizzle, though it was still foundering out. McBride had a large detached house, off the main road out towards Dundrum. It was a two storey, old stone house, with a small front garden and surrounding rough-stone wall. The house was in darkness and there was no car in the driveway. I positioned myself out to the left beside an empty dirt track, and tried to find a way to crouch without soaking myself in the bracken. It was a long, cold wait. About half nine, my perseverance paid off as headlights appeared at the bend in the road, and a car pulled into the drive. McBride got out alone, walked to the door, took out his key and went inside. Lights went on one by one, and then nothing. I waited another fifteen minutes and got up, shook myself down and walked purposefully to the front door. He answered promptly after the first knock. His face was flushed, but seemed to drain when he saw who the caller was.

"Chapman," he said in an empty tone.

"I'd like to have a chat with you, sorry it's late," I said, with a stony stare.

He looked away and rubbed a hand cross his face.

"Surely you had your meeting with Fotheringay, and our business is concluded," he said mechanically, almost without any effort.

"So you've been with Fotheringay," I said.

"Well really, it is no concern of yours who I meet or where I go," he said belligerently. "You have become quite the irritant."

I gently but firmly pressed my hand on to the door frame and leaned close to him.

"You're part of a murder, two murders actually. It's best if you speak with me first. It's really up to you how this thing plays out."

He looked as if he was going to begin an outburst and then stepped back, deflated. He looked to be crumbling, already tired and bruised. I think maybe he had always seemed a bit that way, just that there had been a good enough front before. Maybe there had been a capable, powerful man in there once, but now it was just a shell, a vessel.

"Come through then," he hissed.

He led me through a good-sized hall with three rooms leading off it, and a staircase in front. The walls were filled with watercolours and oils and the same continued into the sitting room. He sat down beside a slate fireplace, a few burning rocks giving off the distinctive peaty smell and some welcome heat. He gestured for me to sit on the leather chair opposite and walked over to a well-stocked crystal drinks cabinet. Setting down whiskeys on the small table between us, he eased himself slowly into his own chair.

Lighting up a thin Camel, he said, "I really have no idea where you are getting these notions from, I mean—"

"Really?" I said abruptly and in a raised, but even voice. "Do we have to do all of that? Let's just get to the bacon."

"You are brazen and quite impossible," he said, reaching for his drink and perhaps looking for some conviction in his voice. "I suppose you think you have some theory to bribe me with."

"No, I don't want anything from you. But, okay, fine. Here's the short version, the headline. And there will be headlines, make no bones about that! And I'm not here to blackmail you either. I'm just trying to figure this thing out, simple as that. It's stupid, I know, but I'm here. And I

know that's quite a problem for you, so you may as well be straight with me now."

He looked at me almost insolently and shook his head, only managing a shrug, no agreement, but no denial either.

"There was no robbery. You and Fotheringay set that up. Then you murdered your brother-in-law. Or maybe Fotheringay actually did it, it doesn't matter much. I'm sure he told you already how I figured it out—get Gallagher steaming drunk, shoot him through the grill. That way you could have had him there a while and once there were more staff on duty, there'd be no need to try and sneak in the main door or through the kitchens. Quite the elaborate touch though, Fotheringay's idea I expect."

I paused dramatically and took a long drink. He let me keep talking, I preferred it that way. He showed no outward emotion, maybe he had none left, or had trouble selecting one.

"It was because of the other murder. Yeah, Robinson in Leicester. I'm sure it probably started off as a scuffle, but whatever went down, he got shot and you and your man Fotheringay were involved. That night, I think you made a choice and probably one you've regretted ever since. You and Fotheringay chose to move on, put it behind you I suppose. But what of Gallagher? Maybe he couldn't live with it and wanted to confess? Maybe he felt it was his fault, stirring up right wing politics and someone dying over it. Or maybe he was blackmailing you? Probably bad enough he ended up marrying your sister. Or maybe you wanted that, to keep him close..."

"I didn't put them together," he spat out suddenly. "It just happened," he said and returned to his smoke and toad-like pondering.

"It just happened—just like the first murder? But not the second, no that was well planned, you didn't have to do that," I pressed.

He looked up at me coldly, silently.

"It must have been tough, talking to him, knowing what you were going to do," I goaded further. "You two must have kept him alive those days, so the body would look right. Kept him tied up? Had to take him to the toilet? Maybe it was that he was blackmailing you, was that it? Maybe he pleaded for his life..."

"Fotheringay, it was Fotheringay," he boomed, rising out of his chair. He sat back down again sharply, dejected.

"Okay, I realise that, but you went along with it all."

"I didn't mean for any of this," he said, offering up a hand in a plea.

He shook his head and blew out a heavy wisp of smoke. "If Gallagher had just been able to keep it together, he wasn't a blackmailer either Mr. Chapman. Since my sister passed," he started quietly, glancing at a photograph on the mantle, "he was lost, remorseful. Fotheringay said he was hardly a living, breathing man anymore anyway, it would almost have been a kindness."

"You don't believe that," I said scoldingly. "I fought people in the war who would have made excuses like that."

We both sat and smoked a moment, the room became smaller.

"So was it Gallagher who shot Robinson? He couldn't convince Robinson of his fascist beliefs, so he killed him over it?"

"No," McBride broke in earnestly. "He wouldn't have hurt anyone, not really. That was Fotheringay. He lost his temper. He was a different man then. Not better, different. I suppose we're all different men now."

All the fight had gone out of McBride.

I heard the click and then saw the door slowly open, but I didn't react fast enough. I don't know if I registered it was Fotheringay in the doorway first, or saw the smoke rise from the gun. A split second later, the crack of the gun sent me moving. I dived around the side of a large antique travelling chest, as the bullet struck McBride in the chest and he let out a guttural groan. I pulled myself further behind the chest and there was a pause, then a second shot. I heard it rip through flesh. He must have taken his time with that one.

"Come out Chapman, I'm not gonna hurt you," Fotheringay called out, in between heavy breaths. I could sense him moving about somewhere around the doorway.

"I'm packing too," I shouted, bluffing, but trying to sound controlled. "I'm coming out shooting."

There were about three seconds where I felt like I turned up to school naked. I didn't know what was going to happen. Then there was a draught and I heard running footsteps on the gravel out the front. I waited another moment and then leapt up. I bolted past McBride, slumped in his chair, and sprinted to the door. I shielded my body around the doorway and watched Fotheringay turn and look me in the eye.

"Give it up Fotheringay. Stark and the whole County Police Force are on their way."

His Browning hung in his hand at his side and his feet almost kept running on the spot. Unexpectedly he raised up his arm and squeezed off a shot. I jumped back towards the stairs and the bullet ricocheted off the door, and shattered the pane in the hall window, making an almighty crash. I crouched down, inching towards the door, and then the footsteps started again. I ran out into the garden, ducking behind trees as I approached the outer wall. The wall then lit up behind too yellow beams and a car engine started abruptly. The tyres gave off a screeching protest as the engine roared and the car sped past the front of the house, heading north. I sprinted back inside, down the hall and back into the living room. From the doorway,

McBride looked almost like he was enjoying an evening doze, except for the awkward way he was positioned, and the red patch oozing on his shirt. I walked across to him. I was now alone in the room.

Chapter Fifty-Five

Regan came out of his house at exactly 10.06 a.m. I wrote it in my book and everything. His substantial body had been poured into a too small tracksuit. I could almost hear it rip, as he got into his car and drove away. I moved out after a few seconds, the now familiarity of this pattern keeping me even. I had popped one of my pills and a cigarette was already lit and hanging out the side of my mouth too. It all helped.

Today we weren't making lots of little stop offs and headed directly to an address in the University area on Wellesley Avenue. I parked up the road a bit and at the other side, where I could watch the house in my rear-view mirror. Regan went into the terrace after first knocking on the door, I couldn't see who had answered. These streets are mostly low grade student housing, but a family also came past me, with two infants on their trikes. A few students wandered past too and an older gent with a cane. It was Sunday morning and quiet, I suppose most of the local population would be asleep in bed, not aware of their hangovers yet.

Buzzzzz.

I nearly jumped out of my skin. It was the walkie talkie.

"Hello?" I said.

"This is Jahn, just checking in. Anything to report?"

"Hello Jahn," I said, turning down Andy Cairns on the stereo and feeling playful. "How's the face?"

"Anything to report?" he repeated.

"I've tailed Regan to a terrace house up near Queen's. He's been there about a half hour. Now, that was a terrace house, not terrorist, just before you get too excited."

"Fine," he said. "Some of our other targets look promising, so just ask for back up if you're certain something is going down. It might be nothing. But keep a close watch."

"Okay," I said and it went dead. "Roger that," I said to no one.

A few minutes later, Regan reappeared. He was now dressed in white overalls, with a few paint stains here and there. These at least looked a more comfortable fit. Behind him followed a second man, short and thin, brown skin, and also in overalls. He closed the door behind them and they crossed the street to get into a white transit van. There was no advertising on it and I noted down the registration. When its engine gurgled into life, we set off again on our procession. The roads were quiet enough, most shops were still not allowed to open on a Sunday until one in the afternoon. It's not like it makes everyone go to church for fucksake, just a stupid Northern Irish inconvenience. I followed them down towards Botanic, past the train station and then out towards Great Victoria Street. We passed the Opera House, City Hall, we might as well have been doing a bus tour. I soon found myself three cars behind them in the queue for the underground parking at Victoria Square.

***

Victoria Square is a four hundred million pound shopping mall, in the centre of Belfast. It was built only a couple of years ago, and it's a mammoth, glass construction, connecting a number of old buildings together. I didn't shop there much because I couldn't afford to. Especially not if I kept taking myself off to hotels. There were plenty of keen shoppers about anyway, getting there early, so I was able to follow them at a distance quite easily. My quarries went past the small fountain and up the escalator and I waited a minute and then did the same. They both carried some kind of tool bags and each had a backpack on their shoulder. They seemed to know exactly where they were headed and on the first floor, they headed to the south side. I tried to look like just another casual shopper as we crossed beneath the zigzag of escalators and the huge glass dome above us. I stopped to look in a window when they went over to the office door, underneath Pizza Hut. They went inside. I waited.

After a few minutes, they emerged again, with a middle-aged man in a suit, sporting a name tag, who then led them hurriedly through the mall. I stood and watched their reflections in the shop window, as they crossed behind me. They then went up the escalator. On the next floor, there are more escalators and then a glass lift. In fact, it looks like Charlie's Great Glass Elevator, though it doesn't go through the roof. What it does do is take visitors to the viewing dome where the escalators cannot get to. The only alternative is a spiral staircase that can take people up the final few meters. When they got to the next floor, they did just that. I looked up cautiously and observed the three men standing silently, as it whisked them up to the dome. I took the various escalators to the final sub floor and started to ascend the stairs myself. I'd have to pass myself off as another shopper, fancying a look at the view.

"They're doing some work up there buddy, closing it off," said a man with his young daughter, coming down in front of me. "They say it'll be back open in the next hour or so."

"Okay, thanks," I replied.

I caught my breath, stood back on the lower floor, and looked up at the dome. *"Could this be the terror attack?"* I asked myself. Could be just some ordinary job Regan is involved in. Or, this could be a purposeful decoy. I rode the escalators back down to the ground floor and picked a spot where I could sit on a bench and make like I was texting, but could observe what was going on above. A few minutes later I watched as the three men descended again, on display in that glass cabinet for all to see. Regan and the second man got out first. The suited man then stepped out and set a 'Closed' sign in front of the elevator, and took out a key and locked the door. The first two nodded and went off. I followed them down to the carpark again and I waited off beside the fountain, betting on them coming back.

Ten minutes later, they passed near to me, struggling to carry a large rectangular object. It was a kind of panel, a metre or so long and about half that wide. It wasn't very thick, but it seemed made of various materials, the top being glass. Up on the viewing floor, I knew there were many of these, connected together on the wall below the glass windows, showing parts of the skyline and what they are. On a clear day, you can see the real structures for yourself behind them. This particular panel showed Stormont, Harland, and Wolff.

I followed them both, back through the mall, my mind racing. Could this be it? Could there be a bomb inside? I suppose these days you could plant one anywhere. Blowing the dome off millions of pounds of local investment, potentially killing hundreds in a busy landmark, would certainly be a good target. I distractedly pretended to check my phone, I didn't have to pretend to be distracted anymore.

The man in the suit met them back at the lift and unlocked it for them. After a few words, they went up. He locked it again and then scuttled off. Was he in on it? Was there anything to be in on? I remember the days when the city centre was surrounded by police check barriers and frequent searches were just part of shopping in Belfast. Incendiary devices could be slipped into jacket pockets in clothes shops, explosives constructed in cars in multi-stories. Maybe it was safer then. Times had changed I supposed. I patted my inner jacket pocket and felt the gun safe inside. I started to take out my walkie talkie but then considered it, changed my mind and put it back in my pocket. I took out my mobile—three new missed calls, two from Mary. I couldn't think about that now. Frig, I really wanted a smoke.

***

When I got to the foot of the stairs, I glanced at the sign in front of the elevator, and then shoved the one at the bottom of the stairs to the side. I started to climb. As I curled around the last steps to the top, I saw their backs, both working at unscrewing one of the panels from the wall. Two steps away, and then they both shot around.

"Closed, it's closed up here," Regan said thickly.

"Oh, sorry about that," I said, but kept on walking. "Flip it's some view," I added, walking on to the centre of the room.

They looked at each other and then both stood up straight.

"Never been up here before, it's some view all right," I repeated, making as if I was taking in the all glass surroundings, still walking forwards again.

"It's closed," Regan urged again, trying to sound affable enough. "It'll be open again in a bit."

I ignored him. "Jeez it's high up here," I said and peered over the top rail. You could look down on the various floors from there and beyond, and it really is high.

I kept smiling and then surveyed them both. Confidence was coming from somewhere. Fuck knows where. Regan was slouching, grimacing slightly. The second man stood awkwardly, nervously, his arms hanging down at his sides.

"So," I said, "what is it you guys are doing up here?"

"We're replacing these maps," said Regan, gesturing hurriedly. "Look, you've got to head on now."

"Just a second," I said and flicked out my radio, my face hardening. "I've got a call here, sorry."

I actually pressed the button down then and really rang through.

"Yeah, yeah, that's grand," I started, talking to no one.

"Hello. What is it Brian?" Jahn said after a click.

"Yeah it's that thing in Victoria Square, the top, that's right."

I looked at them both, then over towards the viewing area, trying to seem indifferent. They both looked away.

"What, what are you talking about?" he said, irritated.

"Yes that's right, just two I think. Okay then?"

"Oh right," he said urgently, comprehending. "Something's going down there, two of them, okay—just try and keep it in hand until we get there."

"Will do, thanks mate," I said and hung up.

"So what, you work here?" said Regan, his voice coarse.

"Something like that," I said and shrugged, keeping my voice and expression level. "I'm just gonna wait around here a while. I've a guy coming round from Health and Safety. Check it out with your boss if you want to."

"What are you— management?" he pushed.

"Police?" asked the second man unexpectedly, and speaking for the first time. It was in a sharp, middle-eastern accent.

"Just go easy," Regan said, turning to the man and raising a hand. He looked worried then.

I glared at the second man, urging him to make his move. It was all the edge I had. All the same, I nearly shit my pants when all of a sudden, he lunged into his bag and pulled out a forty-five. I started to run around the side of the balcony, pulling my own gun out. I saw Regan bend down to his own bag, just as the second guy sent a shot through the elevator glass door. It made an almighty crash and I could almost hear a communal gasp from the shoppers below.

I steadied myself, knowing I had a few seconds to aim, and squeezed off two rounds. The first buzzed off the balcony, before ringing out as it hit the metal girders. The second sank into the man's right arm. He cried out as he dropped his gun and fell to the floor. I started running again, inside my glass rat run, as I clocked Regan begin to aim his own. He went to take a shot and I heard the click of the safety still on. My gun arm was down at my side and I had a split second to think.

I leaped towards him, bringing my arm up, hoping to get a dig in before he could aim again. I made it in time and cracked the metal barrel across his face, above his eyebrow. He bounced back up, bleeding, and pushed me back against the balcony. He got a hand round my throat and pushed my neck over the edge. Both guns had fallen away.

I grappled with him, and managed to get a hand free and push him back a foot. He shot forwards again at me and I grabbed and twisted in one motion, that's all. His momentum was enough to send him flying over the top. He made a dreadful shout as he went over. It was the sound of a tough guy shit scared. There was a sickening thud and then a series of screams from below.

**

I looked over at the other guy. He was out cold, his arm bleeding badly. I bent over him, ripped off a piece of his overalls and wrapped it round his arm tightly. I leaned over the balcony, looking down at where all hell was breaking loose. People were screaming and scrambling around.

Some were running towards and some away. I sat down and leaned my back against the wall and waited.

Chapter Fifty-Six

His eyes were still open, but vacant. I closed them over. I stood up straight and ran my hands through my hair. I was just starting to look around for a telephone when a car door slammed and steps approached again. Stark appeared in the doorway, poised, and with a Service six chamber in his left hand.

"I heard the gunshots on my way up the road and saw a car speed off. Fotheringay?"

"Yeah," I said, relieved to see him, and his gun. "Nice to see a friendly face."

He holstered it and entered the room, his face full of concern, but still composed.

"McBride's dead," I said, gesturing.

"So it would appear," he replied, walking over to the body.

"I got your note and your report," he said, checking for a pulse. "I guess you were right about it all."

"He pretty much told me everything and that was right when Fotheringay burst in and put two slugs in him."

"Okay," he said simply, arching on the balls of his feet. "Do you wanna come?"

"Of course," I said.

We were out in his Ford within seconds and roaring north, along the country road. I lit two cigarettes and passed him one. He took a hand off the wheel and examined it, and then plucked it off me.

"Thanks," he said.

"Where do you think he's headed?" I asked.

"Christ only knows. He's probably just looking to go north and get a bit of distance. Don't suppose he planned on all of this tonight."

"No, probably not," I said, trying not to show I was clinging tightly on to the underside of my seat, as we whizzed round the sharp bends. There was no other traffic and Stark showed he could handle an automobile, as we ate up the miles, passing Castlewellan and heading out towards Dundrum. Soon enough we could make out tail lights every so often, when we got a straight run of road. As we sped along the coastal road, with the choppy night sea to our left, we started to be able to clearly make out the back of Fotheringay's Humber.

Stark put his foot down and we roared past the waves, the mountains to the left racing past like some jerky stop motion animation. As Dundrum town approached, we gained on him, closer, then closer still. We were right behind him, his bumper only yards ahead now. I would see the back of his head, jolting around in the front, as he struggled to keep control.

Stark pushed on and then accelerated further, as we passed the school house. Crash! He rammed into Fotheringay and sparks flew, the Humber swerved once, and then righted itself. Fotheringay sped on and Stark attempted to try and pass on the right, in the other lane. A bend was approaching and Fotheringay started to brake, but much too late. Stark eased off the juice in our car, as we pursued a little behind and off to the right. The Humber was going too fast and some stones and bramble was enough for it to skid and then flip over, hurtling into the lay-by at the bottom of the hill, down beneath the castle.

We swerved and pulled to a stop, twenty yards up ahead. Stark and I looked at one another, and then at disbelief at the car as Fotheringay heaved open a door and clambered out. He stood up, swaying, looking right at us. He pulled out his gun and fired two shots into the front of our car. We both ducked down, and then climbed out each side door, taking cover beneath them. We peered around the cover of the doors, seeing Fotheringay painfully make his way up the path towards the old ruins. Stark stood up, aimed, and sent a couple of rounds in Fotheringay's direction. They echoed off the uneven stone wall, Fotheringay was too far away and with too much cover to be a decent target. The wind was picking up too. Stark eased himself quickly back into his seat and flipped open the little storage compartment. He pulled out a Colt 45, stood again, and handed it to me. I gave Stark a shrug and we both ran towards the hill.

***

*W*e started our way up the slope, staying close to the outer wall for cover. Fotheringay was out of sight and could be hiding anywhere. We passed the bottom tier, some foundation walls remaining, only visible due to the high moon. We approached the upper part of the ruin and the main remains. There is a scattering there of walls and loose parts of the ancient keep. Above it there are some high walls still standing and access from some of the remaining staircases. We continued to the largest part of the outer wall and sheltered behind it, scanning the horizon. A cutting breeze blew through the keep, no less exposed than we were.

"Cover me, I'm going over to the next wall," Stark instructed.

He dipped down low and ran the ten yards between the two. A shot rang out. I could see Stark make it to the wall, the bullet must have sunk into the thick grass beside. I stood up swiftly and fired off two rounds in the direction of where the shot came from. Both hit the bottom of the keep's outer spiral staircase. Stark turned and motioned for me to make a dash up to him. He jumped up again and sent three shots blowing round the stairs. I sprinted across the marsh and dived down beside him, no return fire coming again.

"I'm gonna try and circle round, keep an eye on the entrance. Send a couple in to keep me going," Stark said, *panting. He passed me a handful of bullets and waited while I filled up my chamber.*

"Ready?"

"Good luck," I said.

He made a break and I stood again to send off some covering shots. I had only squeezed one off before Fotheringay stepped out and sent a volley towards me. I got down low beneath the wall, expecting bullets to sink in around me. Nothing came but there was more gunfire. I crawled to the opening of the wall and could see Stark up ahead behind the next wall, clutching on to his leg. I couldn't tell where Fotheringay had gone.

I tried to calm my breathing and pointed my Colt as I watched, looking left, right, over to the keep, towards Stark... Fotheringay! He appeared again, holding his side with one hand, hurt. This time he was up above the wall where Stark was hiding. His other arm was stretched out and he began firing shot after shot, as he walked, like a madman, Stark becoming more exposed with every step. Each bullet made a sickening thud as it ploughed into the grassy bank. I could see Stark having trouble, trying to shuffle further back, buy himself some more time. Fotheringay was opposite me now, some fifteen yards, but illuminated by the heavy moonlight. I leaped up, zigzagging as I ran between the two. One step and I began to fire. Fotheringay stopped and turned, stunned. Five more steps and I sent one whizzing past his ear. He turned and swung his arm ninety degrees towards me. I sent another two volleys. The first missed, the second thankfully dug into his chest. He fell, the gun falling away. A few seconds later and I was alongside him and kicking the gun out of reach. He was alive, he looked at me, those eyes burning brighter than I had seen before. I looked back towards Stark.

"You all right?"

"Yeah, I'll live. What about him?"

I looked down at Fotheringay, my gun hanging tight at my side.

"We'll have to see."

Chapter Fifty-Seven

We said very little in the van, as we drove across town. When Jahn, Hertogen, and the others had arrived, we were out again in minutes, adding myself and now a prisoner too in tow. I let them deal with it all, I'd done enough. I switched off. It was over. I'd done my bit. They were pros, all handled swiftly, and I just let them sweep me along with the other shit they were cleaning up.

The first stop was dropping me off apparently and that would be the end of my service. I can't recall much of what was actually said. I sat in the back, smoking. I didn't ask if I could, didn't think they'd object. *I must remember to get my car*, I reminded myself. It seemed an odd thought to have for the time, everything seemed a bit odd really. I threw my cigarette down on the metal floor and trampled it out.

"I won't be involved in this much further myself," Hertogen said, turning to me. "We're all almost there."

He looked at me thoughtfully, and leaned in.

"Thank you Brian, this will make a big difference."

I nodded, absently.

"Oh, we'll need those from you," he said, gesturing to my pockets.

I pulled out the gun and radio and passed them across. I took out one of my pills and gave that to myself.

***

Then there I was, at my front door, the van speeding away. *What now?* I thought. I'd carried out two murders in the last week and maybe helped prevent a terrorist threat. Now it was all done and dusted and all would be normal? It seemed my killings had all been cleaned away. I put my key in the door and felt all the aches in my body afresh and the flood of general dissatisfaction seemed to fill up my insides. Maybe it'd help with my new book, I thought. What the fuck? How could I just put this all behind me? I opened the door and closed it behind again. I needed to be home, to rest, to sleep. I needed to get back to my WRAP, to look after myself. Then I could try and explain things to Mary. Well, tell her something, obviously not the truth. I sat down on the floor, my head leaning awkwardly against the letter box. I breathed out, long and full. I just sat there. Maybe it would help my writing though, I thought again.

"A kill for Percy?" I said out loud, and let out a nervous laugh.

"A kill for the poet," I said and then jolted sharply when the doorbell sounded behind me.

I shook my head and stood up. I turned around and leafed my fingers through my hair. I must have looked a state. So, what was this, Hertogen changed his mind, come to silence me? ISIS come to make an example of me? An adoring fan come for my autograph?

I opened it. In front of me stood my psychiatrist, Dr. Vine, flanked by two police officers.

"I think you've got the wrong address," I said.

They said nothing.

"Though, I suppose I could be wrong."

Chapter Fifty-Eight

There was no welcome committee again at the hotel. Or I suppose more appropriately, a leaving committee. There was nothing. I carried my little bag for the last time, through the bustling reception. A few staff gave me weary glances, a few just their bland, professional smile. As I approached the front doors, I saw Parsons come out from his office and stand at the front of reception. This time he stared, stony faced.

I stopped and tipped my hat dramatically.

"You're welcome," I shouted.

Stark had sent a car and the officer was nicer to me, a lot nicer. He gave me a genuine and then literal pat on the back. I could get used to these country folk, well some of them anyway.

"How's the leg?" I asked Stark, shaking his hand, as I came into his office.

"It's all right," he said, giving it a shake and sitting down at the desk. I joined him. I lit a cig and he started on prepping his pipe.

"You okay?"

"Fine," I said. "What about our friend?"

"He's not too bad. The wounds were superficial enough. The docs dropped him back here about half an hour ago, we'll send him up to the cells in Belfast this afternoon. You want to see him first?"

"Be rude not to say goodbye," I said, standing.

Another officer led us down the narrow, lime green corridor, and to the only cell in the station. He stuck in the large key and then stepped to the side. Stark chewed on his pipe and gestured for me to go in.

"Take as long as you want."

"I only need a moment."

Fotheringay was lying on the cell bed, bandages on one arm, his torso and both legs. Gone were the sharp suits, replaced by light blue pyjamas. He looked up at me, emotionless, but a smoking kindling still behind the eyes. He tried to look disinterested, or maybe he was.

"I did say I'd be seeing you. I got you a little going away present," I said jovially. "It's an original Percy French too."

I pulled out Percy's letter to me, from my inside pocket, folded over once. I walked across and stood over him, I admit, relishing every moment.

"If you're still alive in about thirty years and get out, hang it above your fireplace."

I slipped it underneath his hand.

***

After all the travelling, it was only a short walk to the Causeway Hotel, but enough for the Antrim rain to beat any heat out of me.

"Hello Maggie," I said.

I'd swear she almost looked pleased to see me.

"Have you seen anything of Mary?"

END

About Simon Maltman

Simon Maltman is a bestselling writer and musician from Northern Ireland. *A Chaser on the Rocks* was his critically acclaimed debut novel, followed by the bestselling collection of shorts: More Faces. Simon is an established musician, performing with his current band The Hung Jury. He lives in Northern Ireland, with his wife and two daughters.

Previous Press:

"The mood is cynical, the wisecracks are plentiful, and the alcohol pours generously… an engaging and unique tale of crime and corruption."
The High Window

"A mystery noir with a twist ending worthy of Dennis Lehane."
The Big Thrill

"An ambitious tale of intrigue set in Ireland, containing two mirror image plots…their investigations end up overlapping in an extraordinary fashion"
Murder Mayhem and More

Social Media Links

Facebook:
https://www.facebook.com/Simonmaltmancrimefiction/

Twitter: https://twitter.com/simonmaltman
@simonmaltman

Blog: http://simonmaltmanblogs.blogspot.co.uk/

Acknowledgements

Thank you to my family and friends for all their support. Thanks to everyone at Solstice. Thank you to all the readers, reviewers, bloggers, fellow writers- you're all brilliant.

If you enjoyed this story, check out these other Solstice Publishing books by Simon Maltman:

A Chaser on the Rocks

Hardened by the mean streets of Belfast, ex-cop Brian Caskey works as a struggling PI. He is isolated and erratic, often losing the battle to maintain his fragile mental health. Caskey escapes the real world by writing crime fiction stories about a 1940's PI investigating mysteries during the Belfast Blitz.

'A Chaser on the Rocks' follows both of these characters in parallel as a 'novel within a novel'. The two stories collide in adramatic conclusion set against the backdrop of The Giant's Causeway.

Simon Maltman has created a modern noir with a new twist, a dash of black humour and a fresh approach and comment onstorytelling.

Previous press for Simon Maltman:

"I'm amazed how a writer can cram so much into such a short space of narrative. You hit the ground running and it's a sprint finish."

Crime Book Junkie

"Praise Satan for Bangorian Simon Maltman."

Irish News

"Long may he continue."

Hotpress magazine

"A compelling tale... a short but snappy read that gives a fresh glimpse into a life of crime and where it can lead you."

Writing.ie

"Those who foresaw the end of the book as artefact with the coming of the digital age hadn't banked on the ingenuity and skill of a number of young writers who are converting the e-book into a work of artistic relevance. Such a case is that of Simon Maltman, a multifaceted writer and musician from Bangor."

Dr David M. Clark

Director Departamento de Filoloxía Inglesa Universidade da Coruña

http://bookgoodies.com/a/B01M039AIQ

Return Run

Professional thief Blake agrees to come in on a nightclub heist outside of Belfast. He doesn't count on a double cross or on stumbling on an old flame and a mess of murder and deceit. Blake was featured recently in the hardboiled story

Riot Score and the press said:

"I'm amazed how a writer can cram so much into such a short space of narrative. You hit the ground running and it's a sprint finish."

Crime Book Junkie
and

"a short but snappy read that gives a fresh glimpse into a life of crime and where it can lead you."

Writing.ie

More Faces ,

More Faces is a crime short story collection from A Chaser on the Rocks author Simon Maltman. The twelve mystery noirs included feature published and previously unpublished stories and all series shorts currently available. Take a journey across Northern Ireland, through the beauty and darkness, with the fresh new voice in Irish Crime Fiction.

"I'm amazed how a writer can cram so much into such a short space of narrative. You hit the ground running and it's   a   sprint   finish."
Crime Book Junkie

"A punchy tale, told plainly, with plenty of pace... of old fashioned thuggery and backstreet skullduggery."
Murder, Mayhem and More

"a snappy read that gives a fresh glimpse into a life of crime and where it can lead you."
Writing.ie

https://bookgoodies.com/a/B06XSLVG4V

54084645R00121

Made in the USA
Middletown, DE
10 December 2017